You Never Get It Back

John Simmons Short Fiction Award

You Never Get It Back

Cara Blue Adams

University of Iowa Press • Iowa City

University of Iowa Press, Iowa City 52242

www.uipress.uiowa.edu
Printed in the United States of America

Cover design by Nicole Caputo
Text design and typesetting by Sara T. Sauers
Printed on acid-free paper

Library of Congress Cataloging-in-Publication Data
Names: Adams, Cara Blue, 1979– author.
Title: You Never Get It Back / Cara Blue Adams.
Description: Iowa City: University of Iowa Press, [2021] |
Series: John Simmons short fiction award
Identifiers: LCCN 2021016971 (print) | LCCN 2021016972 (ebook) |
ISBN 9781609388133 (paperback) | ISBN 9781609388140 (ebook)
Subjects: LCGFT: Short stories.
Classification: LCC PS3601.D36927 Y68 2021 (print) |
LCC PS3601.D36927 (ebook) | DDC 813/.6—dc23
LC record available at https://lccn.loc.gov/2021016971
LC ebook record available at https://lccn.loc.gov/2021016972

For Cam

Contents

For to wish for a hand on one's hair is all but to feel it. So whatever we may lose, very craving gives it back to us again.

—MARILYNNE ROBINSON

You Never Get It Back

I Met Loss the Other Day

I MET LOSS THE other day. I took his measurements. My yellow tape looped around my arm, pins held tight between my pursed lips, I circled him. I measured his thin wrists, his frail neck, his elegantly sloped shoulders. Inseam, sleeve length, the stretch of his forearm: I marked them down in pencil.

He was small. He stood very still as I worked.

His entourage, six thick-necked men, boisterous despite their size, pale handkerchiefs peeking from their dark suits' breast pockets, poked in the nooks and crannies of my shop. They hula-hooped with my skirt wires, nudged one another with my dead mother's ornate wood-handled umbrella, tossed fabric bolts back and forth. Loss looked straight ahead, glancing over only when a crash erupted or someone called to him affectionately.

No one used his name. To them, he was Oss, Lossie, Bonedaddy.

Loss wanted a single-breasted suit, standard issue, merino wool and cashmere with a peaked lapel, but also a prayer robe and a felt cloak. He was going on holiday, he told me. Where, he didn't say.

He produced a tailor's pattern book from 1589. I turned the dry pages. Cutting patterns for clerical robes, silk kirtles, *ropa de letrado*, all given in ells. One ell equals forty-five inches: this is ancestral knowledge, parceled with the family Bible and shears, passed down the years from grandfather to father, father to son. Loss didn't know this. He handed me a conversion table.

"A Savile Row tailor threw me out," he told me.

I told Loss I could give him what he wanted. Ducking the pincushions that whizzed by my head, I flipped through my notebook to a blank page and noted his figuration and posture. I asked him to relax. He nodded, but remained stiff.

As I sketched, I asked Loss about his operation.

Hundreds of people were in his employ, Loss told me. Cataloguing, mostly. Rows of dark heads with neat parts bent over typewriters, clacking away.

"You can't imagine the clamor," he said. "Eventually, it numbs you."

Worse, Loss said, were the administrative meetings. The ceaseless bickering over what constituted loss. Keys, located after four panicky minutes: lost or just misplaced? A coin stolen from an aunt's purse and tossed down a wishing well, a swallowed tooth, an uncle in the grasp of dementia. How are we to gauge? The problems of classification were endless and unyielding.

As he spoke, I saw the warehouses. Each person's losses filed in long skinny drawers. The cavernous echo of clerks' footsteps as they pushed ladders to the far reaches. Each birth a long span of empty drawer that filled. Slow or quick, it always filled.

Each time someone died, Loss told me, the records were purged. In the night, bonfires dotted the perimeter.

I finished. We discussed drape and cut, scheduled a second fitting.

Loss offered to pay in cash. Half up front, half after the skeleton baste. His money roll was enormous. He peeled away crisp hundreds like onion skins.

"No need to pay the second half," I told him.

Loss raised an eyebrow.

"Have a clerk pull my notecards," I said. "I'll take those instead."

Loss shook his head. Beneath his eyes were tiny plum veins. "They'd fill a wheelbarrow. Take the money. Buy something. Only on Wall Street can you trade with your losses."

I hefted the heavy felt in my hands. Loss reached out and stroked it. I waited. He said nothing.

I waited some more.

"Okay," Loss said finally, "but just a sampling. And duplicates only."

We shook.

After he left, I oiled my shears. I marked the thin, brown-speckled pattern paper with Loss's measurements. Scotch-taped to the window, the paper shone like stained glass. In my hands, the fabric came apart and then together again in Loss's shape. Not alchemy, but close, I thought. Close.

At the appointed hour, Loss returned. His entourage waited outside, kicking empty cans into the gutter. In the gray light they looked at once thuggish and impossibly young.

During the fitting, Loss was patient. He stretched out his arms like a child playing airplane, reached for the sky, ducked and feinted. A few minor adjustments were agreed upon, but everything fit him beautifully.

I promised him the finished garments sewn up tight as a shroud in ten days' time. Loss nodded, said his assistant would collect them, and then reached inside his jacket and handed me three manila cards.

Each card was annotated in an old-fashioned typeface. My name appeared at the top left, the series number at the top right. Dead center was the list. *Gold filling*, the first card began. *Train schedule. Yellow slicker just before the sky opened. Bearings (ball). Bearings (sense of). Orange rind. Tax forms.*

Things I couldn't remember losing. Things I'd missed all my life.

"Sure you don't want the money?" Loss asked. "You could buy another slicker."

"No thanks," I said.

Loss shrugged. I had the sense he'd seen it before: people unwilling to let go of what was gone.

Before he let himself out, Loss brushed my cheek lightly with the back of his knuckles—just the way you always would. Just the way I know you will again, after you walk barefoot down the dirt drive to your mailbox, slit open my envelope and find these cards, after you finally hold in your hand what for all those years I could never bring myself to show you.

· I ·

You Never Get It Back

A PARTY WAS BEING HAD, and Kate agreed to go. The party would be held in Cambridge, a five-hour bus ride away from southern Vermont, where she was working part-time in a lab and living with her mother this first year out of college to save money and think about what kind of future she might want. It was a New Year's Eve party. With the arrival of a new millennium came a legitimate, historic-feeling reason to panic or celebrate, depending on one's inclination; the whole world was gearing up. Her old college roommate Esme called to invite her on December 30, and because Kate was fighting with her boyfriend, with whom she had planned to spend New Year's Eve, she said yes, though not without hesitation. But Esme begged; she didn't want to go alone. She promised Kate that this party would be fun and cheap and attended by Harvard Law School students, including Esme's ex-boyfriend, Paul. Kate and Esme could crash at his studio in the densely populated, Harvard-dominated neighborhood behind the law school if a better option failed to present itself.

"Both of us? It won't be awkward?" Kate asked, and Esme assured Kate that she and Paul had a friendly relationship and that each regarded the other with platonic affection but had moved on, going so far as to suggest perhaps, just maybe, if this other thing wasn't working out, Kate might be interested in him. No, no, Kate said, never going to happen, but Esme persisted, saying that Kate would like Paul. He had grown up in a single-parent household in a little town outside Albuquerque, lived in a trailer. Was determined to rise from the lower middle class to the upper middle class.

"Some men in his position would want to be rich," Esme told her, "but he's not greedy. He wants a nice life, that's all."

Was Esme herself still interested in Paul? Kate couldn't tell.

She made a noncommittal noise.

"You're his type, Kate," Esme continued. "Smart, brunette, with a working-class background. I was too blonde for him. He called me Princess. He hated that I grew up in a bedroom with white carpet."

Kate arrived at South Station from Vermont before Esme's Amtrak train came in from the posh town in rural northern New Jersey where she had grown up. Esme was spending the winter holidays there with her parents, a VP at a pharmaceutical agency and a real estate agent who were both now semiretired. Esme considered them her best friends. In her mind they led audacious, iconoclastic lives. "In the eighties, when my father was a lowly bench chemist," she would say, "my mother outearned him!" They liked to drink and throw catered parties.

Kate towed her luggage from the bus station through the chill wind of the concrete-walled outdoor walkway to South Station's main building, which housed the train station. Waiting in the train station's warm, brightly lit food court, Kate ordered a pepperoni slice from Sbarro and ate the slice with a plastic knife and fork to make it last. An hour to spend here, at least. But she had been the one to suggest she wait. Go along to Cambridge when you arrive, Esme had said. Paul will be happy to see you.

Kate wished she had a cell phone. If the train was delayed, how would she know? She would have to ask the desk agent.

The big clock by the black arrivals board read 2:07 p.m. Esme's train was due in at 3:05 p.m. She read a back issue of *Structure* until 2:55 p.m. and went to the platform to stretch her legs.

Outside, the sky was already darkening. A light snowfall drifted down from the flat gray vault, the wind picking up the dry flakes on the platform and eddying the snow in small twists like a peel of lemon in a cocktail. The pale light had a muffled quality, as if strained through white gauze. Would the party be fun? She gave it a fifty-fifty chance. A small regret moved through her; she would prefer to be in New York with Michael. But he hadn't called, and what could she have done, gotten the ski resort's address from his mother and shown up unannounced? No. And anything was better than sitting home on New Year's Eve, worried and humiliated and preparing to break up with him unless he had a truly dazzling explanation for his behavior.

Two trains arrived on parallel tracks. Passengers disembarked into the cold air, stamping their feet and chafing their hands.

"Roomie!" Esme's voice called from behind her. Esme liked to call her this, as if to reinforce the source of their unlikely bond. Their junior year at Williams, they'd roomed together, matched up by the housing office when Kate's freshman- and sophomore-year roommate transferred to Yale and Esme transferred in. Before going their separate ways senior year, Kate to a co-op and Esme to an off-campus apartment, they'd grown unexpectedly close. Kate listened to Esme's romantic worries and reassured her about her academic papers, which Esme gave to Kate to read, and, after hearing her responses, relentlessly revised into perfection. Esme, in turn, took offense on Kate's behalf when she felt Kate had been slighted and insisted Kate stand up for herself when a professor failed her on an exam when she was in the infirmary with strep throat. She helped Kate with money, too. She had bought Kate's second-semester schoolbooks on her parents' credit card, knowing the books' expense was a hardship and insisting her parents didn't mind when Kate tried to refuse what seemed too large a gift. And now, unlikely a pair though they were, they stood greeting each other in South Station on the cusp of a new millennium.

Small and bird-boned, Esme struggled along the wet platform with an oversized Chanel duffle bag. She dropped the bag to embrace Kate. The two women let out a joint shriek of happiness, or a performance of happiness, and Esme said, "Hi, hi, hi, oh, you look great," as Kate said, "You're here!"

A businessman in his forties trailed Esme.

"Kate, this is Duncan," she said triumphantly, pulling away and turning to acknowledge him. "Duncan, my brilliant roommate Kate."

Esme collected men. She was good at it.

"Nice to meet you," the man said. To Esme: "Where are you headed? I can give you a hand with that bag."

The businessman walked them to the Red Line. He left the bag at the turnstiles, hoisting it over to Esme after she passed through the steel arms. "Can you get it? I can carry it to the platform if you'd like," he said, nodding toward the glass window behind which sat a T official to indicate he could buy a token.

"No need," Esme said. "But thank you."

Kate dragged her own dingy roller bag, taking care not to dirty it further. The pink fabric showed all stain. The wheels were wet from slush. Snow clung to the bag, and as Esme took the man's card and made a general promise to call if she found a free minute for lunch while she was in town, Kate brushed away the white accumulation with her bare hand, the warmth melting the snow so the fabric grew damp, pink deepening to a dusky rose.

Their first semester as roommates, the two had seen each other little. Esme had spent many weekends away in New York City, visiting Paul, who worked for a public policy think tank. He was five years older. Kate had never met him; he and Esme had split up that November because Esme had fallen for a lanky, wealthy member of the lacrosse team—though really, Kate suspected, the problem had been Esme's jealousy of Paul's ex-girlfriend, a model, and Paul's resistance to Esme's plans, which involved moving to Princeton and settling down into a life like her parents' in a community that seemed to demand one strive for more while pretending to think of oneself as a success. Kate was busy with schoolwork, trying to salvage a faltering attempt to double major in physics and chemistry, a choice she was beginning to doubt was a good one, though it had qualified her for several scholarships.

But that spring the two shared an English class. Kate enjoyed the short stories the professor assigned. She tended to sympathize with the women in these stories, and she tired of the boys in the class making comments like "She's so self-pitying" about a girl dating a married man, even though the girl blamed only herself and was self-deprecatingly funny about her regrets, or "I'd be out of there" about a grieving wife mourning a stillborn baby and shaken by a carjacking who began to suffer an extreme fear of break-ins. Or about the bullying, patronizing, passive-aggressive young American man in "Hills Like White Elephants," a character even Hemingway didn't much seem to like as he, the young man, pushed his girlfriend, Jig, into having an abortion: "He's being rational. He just wants a straight answer, but she's being so *emotional* about it." "What does she mean when she says, 'You never get it back?' " one went on. "She hasn't even *lost* anything." The professor, a new assistant professor about the age of the fictional grieving wife, smiled when the boys made these comments and left it to the girls in the class to take up the cudgel for empathy, for feminism. Esme was unafraid in this regard. Her good looks and intellectual confidence shielded her from the boys' dismissal or ridicule. She had recently been introduced to critical theory, too, and she liked to talk about homosocial triangles, and because no one knew what she meant, they were cowed into silence. This had interested Kate.

Kate suspected that Esme regarded her, with her scholarship and work-study job in the lab and what Esme might call her disadvantaged background, as a charity case. But despite this, Kate felt an affection for her; Esme was smart and could be generous. Kate spent the first two months of the fall semester evading Esme's questions about her family, choosing not to disclose how much they'd struggled after her father left, but when her mother called one night, worried about money and in fact sounding suicidal and Esme overheard the conversation and the subsequent call to Kate's aunt, the plea for intervention, she was tactful and compassionate. The fact that she regarded Kate as exotic held an appealing innocence.

Riding the T to Harvard Square, Esme told Kate about graduate school. She was studying English at Stanford, a decision over which she had agonized; accepted at all the top schools, she'd gone into a tailspin and called Kate crying, barely able to choke out, "Harvard and Yale are both *so good*, but the theorist I most want to work with is Terry Castle." Kate had been torn between sympathy and distaste. Esme was so afraid, beneath her confidence, of failing. Once at Stanford, she asked to be assigned to the medical school dorm so she could meet a doctor. She reported without irony that her mother's advice was to sit on the medical school steps reading a book. "But the dorms are better," she'd said, "more casual. More points of contact." Kate thought Esme should go to business school. Forget teaching; her mind was tuned to strategy. She would perhaps be best suited to running the free world.

"I talked to my advisor last week, and he thinks I should learn German and write my dissertation on this one medieval dramatist named Hrotsvitha. I could focus on how her plays relate to our gendered conception of innocence, using Eve Sedgwick as a lens text."

"Do you want to learn German?" Esme had begun as a Henry James scholar; her true fondness was for romantic stories of American girls abroad.

Esme shrugged. "Sure. My advisor says it's my best chance at being competitive for jobs."

"What happened to James?"

"He's overdone."

Kate knew little about PhDs in the humanities and the academic job market. Still, it struck her as silly to focus on an area in which you weren't all that interested if you were going to study the topic for five or more years and go on to teach it.

About Esme, Michael had remarked, "She learns things to have information to lord over you in conversation, not because she actually wants to know." He was an economics major in his senior year at Cornell and planned to work in finance; he believed money was power, and that was what he wanted. His view of the world was unduly cynical, Esme frequently remarked to Kate, but too often he was proven right.

"How is UMass?" Esme asked.

Kate worked twenty hours a week in a lab on campus researching DNA. Or rather, as a technician in support of the postdocs and lead scientist who did the research. Her increased work-study hours and flagging grades had forced her to drop the chemistry major in her senior year, minoring instead, so after graduating with her physics degree, she'd sought research experience. It was an hour drive, and she shared the car with her mother, so she scheduled herself for the longest days possible. Her job was to help carry out crystallographic analysis by cleaning and prepping equipment, tedious but necessary tasks. She was saving for a deposit on an apartment and applying to full-time jobs in Boston and New York.

"You know—fine. The work is a little rote, but it's going to be until I get an advanced degree. It's good to be around these scientists and see how they got where they are and what they like and don't like about the job."

"And Michael? What a shit."

"I know. But maybe he has a good reason."

"There is no reason good enough."

Kate knew Esme was right. Things with Michael were complicated, though; he made her laugh, and he was genuine and angry in a way she liked. Why anger drew her she didn't know. Esme located men she could control; Kate chose men she could not. Perhaps it had to do, she speculated, with Esme's love of constructing a good story, as opposed to her own curiosity about the results of an experiment.

By the time they arrived at Paul's building, darkness had fallen. The wind gusted. Kate could swear the temperature had dropped ten degrees in the fifteen minutes between when they emerged from underground at the Harvard Square station and now. A winter storm advisory was in effect, Esme said; they were lucky to have made it to Paul's before the snow began in earnest. She pressed his buzzer, holding it an extra second as Kate shivered. The wind whipped her hair into her mouth. Her nose ran. They waited. Esme pressed the buzzer a second time and a loud buzz issued forth. The door lock clicked open.

The women climbed a narrow, dim flight of stairs, bags bumping behind them as a man Kate assumed was Paul opened a door five flights above and waited in the doorway.

"Sorry!" he called down. "I don't have my keys and it'll lock behind me."

"That's fine," Esme called up, giving a brittle laugh that said it obviously wasn't. Kate paused on the second-story landing, rearranged her grip on the bag. Esme stopped behind her. "My duffle isn't too heavy," Esme called, "but Kate has an actual suitcase. Do you want to find your keys?"

"Of course," he said. "Hold on a sec."

Esme set her bag on the landing and waited for Paul. He retrieved his keys and bounded down the stairs. He hugged Esme, who responded with tepid enthusiasm until he lifted her in the air, at which point she relented and seemed pleased by the flattering attention. After lowering her, he shook Kate's hand. His grasp was warm. Now disarrayed, his longish brown hair fell across his forehead. She took in his undeniable good looks: pleasantly crooked nose that might once have been broken, a mouth that suggested good humor and intelligence. When he smiled at her, she wanted to smile back.

"Here," he said. "I'll get these," and he lifted the two bags and carried them up the remaining three flights of stairs in the effortless way that surprised Kate, even though she knew to expect it from men. They were stronger. And yet it was hard to look at her bag and see a thing that could be easy to lift. It necessitated looking at a suitcase and seeing in its place a lighter object: a pillow, a microscope, a slide. She envied that ability to act on the world.

Paul wore gray sweatpants and a T-shirt, and she could see Esme examining this choice critically. Esme liked her men well dressed. For holidays she gave them clothes she wanted them to wear and then complimented them encouragingly for wearing the sweaters and button-downs, soliciting other people's approval. "Don't you think Marcus looks handsome in this shirt?" she would ask friends, or "Doesn't this lilac make Jake's eyes look *so blue*?" and what could one say but yes? The men Esme dated usually seemed to expect this and were happy to humor her; the ones who resisted didn't last long. Such agency, to shape a person to your will and to refuse them if they did not yield. Paul had refused to yield.

The studio was small but neat. Paul put their bags by a faded maroon futon couch. A television opposite the couch provided a focal point; beside it stood a small bookshelf with legal books. Adjacent to the kitchen, a desk was wedged in the dining nook where a kitchen table should go, a green-shaded lamp emitting soft light.

Paul went to get them drinks. "Beer or wine?" he asked the women. "I haven't been properly domesticated," he added, nodding to the desk. "I eat on the couch if I eat here, which is rare. But please note, I did clean up for you two."

Esme wandered toward the kitchen, where Paul stood uncorking a bottle of wine, and peeked through the open door to the bedroom. Kate joined her, hanging back a little. The studio was not a true studio; in fact, it was two rooms, though the bedroom was closet-sized. "Clean sheets," he said. "Look, there's even a decorative pillow. The futon's murder. I'll take it. Or we can all sleep in the bed."

At this Esme turned to him and said, "*Someone*'s getting ahead of himself." Paul laughed an easy, perhaps flirtatious laugh. "Baby doll," he said, "since you broke my heart I haven't even allowed myself to dream of you. You ruined me, you know. Gutted me like a fish."

"Please," she said.

"She's a heartbreaker, this one," he called to Kate.

Emerging from the kitchen area with two glasses of red wine he distributed to the women, he smiled and announced, "I'm going to hop in the shower. The day got away from me. I thought we'd grab a bite to eat before the party. There's a great cheap place around the corner. You two like Middle Eastern?"

Mollified by the flirtation, Esme said yes. Kate was relieved. Cheap was good. Each week, she saved as much of her small paycheck as she could so she might afford a deposit on an apartment, but most of the money went to cover her portion of the telephone bill and bus fare to see Michael, and to her mother, who insisted Kate didn't have to pay rent but who appreciated the help. Her disability check only went so far, and after the second month without enough heat, Kate started chipping in, even though her mother protested; they both knew it was the only reasonable option. Esme enjoyed nice restaurants and tended to suggest expensive places. Worries about money she met with "This is the one time we're here" or "We work hard. We *deserve* this" or "In five years whatever we spend on this meal is going to seem like such a pitifully small amount of money," which Kate sincerely hoped was true.

She began to feel guilty at dinner. Esme and Paul caught up over falafel and hummus, Paul occasionally asking Kate a question about herself to draw her into the conversation—what had she studied at Williams? And what did she do now? If she was in Boston looking for jobs, she could stay with him; he might even have a lead for her on a position at an MIT lab—and she was appreciative but distracted. It had been four days since she had spoken with Michael. Kate normally took a bus to see him on holiday breaks. His parents lived in Westchester. The Greyhound went from Brattleboro to Port Authority, where he would pick her up. Before Christmas, they had planned to meet in New York on New Year's Eve, watch the ball drop live in Times Square on this historic occasion, but after their Boxing Day fight, he went on an impromptu skiing trip with his friends and did not leave a telephone number; three times, she'd spoken with his mother and left him messages, all unreturned. Angry as she was, a small part of her held out hope. What if Michael had a good reason for not calling from the ski cabin, and he called her house in Vermont to explain himself and to arrange to pick her up in New York or to offer to drive to Vermont for New Year's, and he couldn't get her? Her mother did not like to answer the phone.

"Esme," she said quietly, when Paul was in the restroom, "can I leave Michael your cell number? In case he needs to reach me?"

"Absolutely not," Esme said. "He needs to sweat."

Paul, returning, smiled warmly at both women and asked what he'd missed. To Kate's embarrassment, Esme gave him a rough outline of her romantic situation, emphasizing that Michael was not good enough for Kate, was not fit to buy her dinner, let alone date her. "This is inexcusable, right?" she concluded. "She needs to end it. And we need to help her. Do you have any cute friends?"

"Plenty," Paul said affably.

"And you're single yourself."

"Esme," Kate said sharply, more sharply than she had intended. She'd meant it to sound like a groan, like, please, not more of this, to diffuse the tension, when instead she sounded like a person whose secret interest had been revealed. Paul didn't appear to notice. He had a way of noticing small things when they might add to a person's comfort—her silence at the table—and not noticing them when they were embarrassing or awkward, a form of social grace she liked.

"What?" Esme said. "You two have a lot in common."

"Do we?" Paul asked. He waved to the waitress and ordered baklava.

"You both have single mothers."

"That isn't so rare," Kate said.

"You're smart, admirable people. You grew up in single-parent households, worked hard, and succeeded." Esme paused, considering. "Remember when we went camping?" she asked Paul. "And we ran out of water? And the nearest place to get water was three miles away?"

"Sure," he said.

"And you hiked there and back to get the water."

"You had a blister. I shouldn't have let you go on a long hike in new boots."

Kate could imagine this scenario well. Esme hated the outdoors, though she liked to claim she was woodsy. She would begin a project like this, a hike, a camping trip, and quickly plead illness or injury to curtail it, returning with a glorious story of triumph over adversity. Paul's voice held no animosity, though, and he looked at Esme in a protective, affectionate way that suggested his flirtation might be a test.

"See?" Esme said. "Kate's just like that. She'd hike six miles without complaining."

And Esme wanted to establish his interest and turn him away.

"You have a work ethic," Kate said. "It's not the sole territory of us children of single mothers."

"Sure, I work hard," Esme agreed. "But you and Paul *overcame* things."

The baklava arrived. Paul distributed it among the three of them. Esme checked her phone, and he winked at Kate, a fast, subtle indication he knew what Esme implied was insulting and ridiculous and that he felt no need to let Esme know this. She felt grateful. Of course he knew; he'd dated Esme. She could relax. She didn't need to debunk these ideas. Esme would be Esme and that was okay. She and Esme were different, and those differences were in some ways unbridgeable: Esme, with her vacations in Europe and her childhood bedroom with the canopy bed and white carpet and private, pink-wallpapered bathroom; Kate, with her summers spent working as a dishwasher at a local restaurant and her futon mattress on the floor of the uninsulated back room in her mother's drafty, government-subsidized house.

• • •

They stopped at a package store near the Middle Eastern restaurant to buy liquor to bring to the party. Paul paid, as he had paid for dinner —"You're my guest," he protested when Kate reached for her wallet; Esme made no such gesture—and, at Esme's request, they returned to Paul's apartment so Esme could change. To this suggestion Paul said, "You look great. Kate, you too." But Esme said she felt underdressed seeing partygoers in the streets of Cambridge, men in blazers and women braving the snow and cold in cocktail dresses and heels. At Paul's she put on a sparkly blue shift, against which her white-blonde hair glowed, and delicate gold shoes; Kate, having brought nothing so dressy, wore dark jeans and a black top.

Snow fell faster outside. Esme, after insisting she could walk to the party in her stilettos, observed meaningfully two blocks into the walk that the sidewalks were icy, and Paul, with infinite patience, said not a word. He put up a hand and hailed a taxi and opened the door for the women.

As the taxi swerved through narrow Cambridge streets, throwing slush onto the sidewalks from the icy puddles, Esme and Paul laughing and taking sips from a flask Paul had produced from his jacket, Esme clutching Paul's arm dramatically at turns, Kate borrowed Esme's phone and called Michael's parents' house. His mother answered in Korean and, hearing Kate's voice, switched to English. Her voice was warm but hesitant, halting. She attended a Korean church, maintained friendships with Korean women in her neighborhood, and spoke with her husband in Korean at home. He'd been a doctor in Korea and now ran three bodegas in Trenton and East Orange and was fluent in English, but she had no reason to be. This was why she persisted in speaking to Michael in Korean, though he responded in English, neither at home in the other's first language.

"Michael not here," she said, and Kate explained that she wanted to leave a new telephone number for when he returned. She was staying at a friend's apartment in Boston, she told his mother, careful to keep references to this friend gender-neutral.

Their fight had been about how to spend New Year's Eve. Michael had said they couldn't go out with his friends to the Korean bottle clubs they frequented in the city because she was white, that even if he could get her into a club, which was unlikely, she would dislike these friends, a clique of wealthy Korean and Korean American college students she hadn't met once in the two years she and Michael had dated. These friends were materialistic, he said, obsessed with fashion; the women were dependent upon the men for money and gauged love this way. The female half of one couple did not carry credit cards or cash or any form of currency when traveling; she simply expected her boyfriend to pay. In return he ordered for her: salads, because she was plump. "You'd hate the whole scene," he told Kate, and he was probably right. Michael wasn't like this in most respects; he wore ratty old T-shirts and admired her independence and ambition, but he liked the comfort of being around them. "So you'll always have two lives," she'd said, "including one in which I can't participate?" He had never failed to be honest in her presence, but she wondered how, and whether, he talked about her to these friends. "Yes," he'd said after a pause. "I guess that's right."

"Okay, I tell him," his mother said on the phone now, "bye," the way these calls usually ended.

"Happy New Year," she managed to get in. She wished she spoke Korean so she could talk in an open way with this woman, whom she liked a lot, though they communicated mainly in gestures and smiles and in their familiar call-and-response upon seeing each other: You look thin, his mother would say with a mixture of admiration and concern; have you been sick? No, she would say, I haven't been sick. And his mother would smile and say, Good, good, very thin, very nice.

Hanging up, Kate saw Esme and Paul looking at her expectantly.

"Not home," she said.

"Good," Esme said. "You've done your duty, and you didn't even have to talk to the miserable bastard. If he calls, break up with him. From here on in you can consider yourself free."

"Don't pick up if he calls tonight," Paul said, reasonably. "It's hard to break up with someone on New Year's Eve. It's too emotional. Have fun at the party and have the conversation in a few days."

That she was not necessarily planning to break up with Michael she didn't say. She should end it, she knew. She should. But she missed him. He was funny and honest. Because of his sense of outrage at the world's unfairness, his alienation, he could voice what she herself couldn't, could hold others responsible in a way her own sympathies and, yes, her own fear prevented her from doing. She wanted to hear his caustic take on Esme's behavior toward Paul, his assessment of this party to which they were headed. She wanted him to make her laugh.

The Harvard Law student hosting the party had bought his loft upon starting school, Paul said. His name was Amir, and his father owned four hotel chains based in Florida. Amir was twenty-seven years old and regarded law school as good preparation for serving on the board when he turned thirty, which was the family plan. The family plan also involved Amir's coming into a good deal of money beyond his generous trust fund once he proved he could conduct himself responsibly, the standard of which was not failing out of Harvard Law.

But the plan for the night had little to do with responsible corporate stewardship. Nothing, in fact. Quite the opposite: irresponsible individual hedonism. And why not enjoy being young and wealthy as the century came to an end, Paul asked? Why not go on enjoying these things as long as possible, in fact? Until the youth and the money ran out?

"We like to encourage Amir to squander his trust fund," Paul said. "Not that it's tough to do. He spends money like it's a hobby. At least when he's penniless, he'll have his law degree to fall back on."

But the money would not run out, Kate felt sure—not for Amir or people like him. There was too much of it, too much to burn in one life.

The loft was brick walled and high ceilinged and spacious, a huge room with large windows that looked out on the dark Charles River. Strands of white lights twinkled, nets strung across the ceiling. A staffed bar had been set up in the back. The bartenders wore gray vests over white shirts, sleeves cuffed. Hip-hop pumped through the professional-grade sound system, bouncing off the brick. The party was more adult than she had expected, not the standard postcollegiate affair with people congregated in the kitchen, drinking from plastic cups, the young men reminiscing about college, the young women overdressed and attempting more elevated conversation.

Paul went to get drinks. He greeted a male classmate on his way to the bar and waved the friend over to them, pointing out the two women. The friend pushed through the crowded room. Esme and Kate stood at the outskirts of the dancers, where groups of people clustered, talking.

The friend wore old-fashioned wire-rimmed glasses. Blinking in a slowed-down fashion that suggested he'd had a few, he peered at Kate and Esme, saying by way of introduction, "So what do you think? Is this the end of late capitalism?" He held a glass of whiskey and rattled the ice cubes, smiling appraisingly.

"Undoubtedly," Esme said.

"I hope not," Kate said. "We just got here."

Paul emerged with the drinks, a champagne cocktail for Esme and gin and tonics for himself and Kate.

"It's snowing outside," the friend said, gesturing to the gin and tonics that Paul and Kate held.

"Always so literal, aren't you, Rand?" Paul said.

"Order is the backbone of society."

"Kate wanted one," Paul said. This was true. She had not realized it was an odd thing to request.

"A contrarian," Rand said. "I like that in a woman."

"What happened to order being the backbone of society?" Paul asked.

"I'm worried about ruffians like you," Rand said with a smile, "not girls like this."

He was older and had the bloated look of a banker. Too many late nights at the desk, too many dinners with clients.

Esme laughed, making eye contact with Rand, who smiled back. She didn't like it when Kate was the focus of attention for too long. She liked to direct attention to Kate, like an MC, and quickly reclaim it.

"And you," Rand said to Esme, "champagne already? Midnight's an hour off."

Paul waved to a group of classmates, ushered them over, introduced everyone: Miriam, Alice, and Jonathan. Hands were shaken, names repeated. Jonathan was tall and fair, with an athletic build, perhaps of Scandinavian origin; he spoke with a trace of an accent. The women were both South Asian. Their eyes were rimmed with dark kohl-like eyeliner, their hair dark, their clothes dark, and they spoke in murmurs. The music grew louder.

Esme's gaze switched to Jonathan, a runner. "I run too," she said. They began to discuss the best way to stretch. Kate asked Miriam what she did. Alice drifted off to get a drink. "I'm in school with these jokers," Miriam said. Her hair was cropped in a pixie cut, like a sixties icon. "But they want to be corporate assholes and I want to do civil rights law."

"You'll marry one of us corporate assholes and we'll bankroll your conscience," Rand remarked, overhearing.

"I said assholes. I didn't say unattractive," Miriam responded. To Kate, she said, "You're here with Paul?"

"Yes—or, well, we're staying with him, Esme and I. Esme knows him. I don't yet, not really."

"Ah," Miriam said. "He's one of the good ones, as you'll see."

"I do my best," Paul said, turning from the conversation he'd been having. "Miriam, Kate is a scientist. She's going to figure out the secrets of the human genetic code and save us from ourselves. Kate, as you may have heard, Miriam is going into civil rights. You two will redeem us all."

Esme laughed at this, the rustle a dry leaf scraping across concrete. Kate looked away from Paul's smile. She was beginning to like him, but she did not want to cross Esme. Female friendship was a complicated business.

Before midnight the music dropped. A plasma TV tuned to the ball in Times Square came on, and the partygoers gathered and chanted the countdown. Champagne flutes were passed around but didn't reach their group in time. Paul put his arms around Kate and Esme and pulled them in close—"Three! Two! One!" the crowd cried—and at midnight, he kissed each on the cheek, first Esme and then Kate, the touch of his lips warm and soft. Kate felt so lonely in that moment. What was Michael doing? Who was he kissing? She couldn't imagine him being unfaithful, but no word for four days; surely it was over. It had to be.

They had never not spoken for so long, even after their worst fight, which had taken place six months earlier in New York on a hot July night. Her bus had arrived at Port Authority at 2 a.m. on a Friday, or, well, a Saturday, and he'd been late to pick her up. The crowd at that hour was rough; she'd gone to the public restroom to find two women fighting and a third apparently passed out in a stall, dirty white sneakers visible beneath the stall door, and had left without using the bathroom. She'd waited for Michael on the street corner for forty-five minutes. Anticipating her displeasure, he was in a bad mood. When the man at the parking lot charged him more than he'd been told he'd have to pay, he argued. "I have cash," she'd said, and he'd snapped, "That's not the issue."

The parking lot attendant was a fiftyish-looking black man. She felt bad for him; he seemed reasonable, weary, as he explained to them that the electronic system would not allow him to charge less and that if the owner found less in the cash register, he would be accused of stealing.

Michael paid the amount without speaking. Leaving, he slowed at the speaker and spat on the gray mesh cover. "Motherfucking—," he called, followed by a word she almost could not believe she'd heard, and sped off.

She had been stunned into silence. He interpreted this silence correctly as anger, disgust, disavowal. He had black friends; in the two years they'd dated, he had never said anything she could remember interpreting as racist. "I know what you're thinking. Say it," he said. "Kate, say it." She couldn't. What did she need to say, she found herself wondering, to separate herself from those words? She could not speak.

"I'm going to keep driving until you talk," he said. He drove around the silent, dark suburbs outside the city. The minute she spoke, she knew she would become the target of his anger. She could not coax any words from herself. He spoke instead; he said she could not know what it was like to grow up in a household of Koreans who were mocked and shut out by white society, polite though it appeared on the surface, and who feared black people, who worked in black cities and were targets of racially motivated violence. "I know you had it hard," he said, "but there are some things you will never understand." This was true. She could not know. She was so tired. The anguish and rage in his voice flickered as a heat inside her, died. "Please talk to me," he'd said, "please." And when she still did not speak, he pulled over and stopped. "Get out of the car," he said, and she had, she'd watched him drive away and begun walking, wondering which doorbell she should ring, debating whether it was better to say her car had stalled or to confess the truth.

When he'd come back for her, he'd broken down crying, the only time she'd seen him cry. He apologized. For what he'd said to the man, for leaving her. He promised he would work on himself. He begged her forgiveness and agreed when she pointed out that hers was hardly the most important forgiveness to ask. This went on for hours, and though she had wanted to end it then, had seen the end, she had at last capitulated. And after that, things were better between them, as if in the fight a tension had lifted.

Five minutes after midnight, Esme's phone rang. She had set it on a nearby table. Rand answered. "Who?" he yelled. "Wait, I think so. What does she look like?"

It was him. Of course.

Taking the phone, she said, "Hello?" in a way she hoped was matter-of-fact, not elated, not angry.

"Where are you?" he said. He was furious. "Who answered the phone?"

"A friend of a friend," she said. "We're at a party." She felt not victorious but low.

"Where?" he demanded.

"Cambridge, somewhere. We're staying in Cambridge."

She found a quiet corner by the loft's enormous windows, which revealed a glinting snowfall. The veil of snow made the street look dim and mysterious, a face glimpsed across a subway platform before a train arrived. Beyond the trees lay the river's shadowy, silvered curve.

"Who are you staying with?"

"Where have you been? I've been calling for four days."

"We were at the ski cabin, and there was no landline and no one's cell phone worked up there. The cold killed the car battery."

"Why didn't you invite me?"

"You wouldn't have been comfortable. Trust me."

"You couldn't call from the lodge?"

"I should have called, I know. I'm sorry. I was so focused on getting the car fixed, and I thought it would be done in time to call you this morning to make plans." This made no sense to her—surely he could have called? And waiting until the day of New Year's Eve to make plans seemed absurd—but perhaps it was because she'd been drinking. He sounded so rational.

The crowd jostled closer as more people began to dance. She had been sipping a whiskey, and her head felt detached from her body, a balloon she held by a string. Miriam was bending to take off her heels, the kohl around her eyes smudged, a hand on Rand's arm to steady herself. Kate overheard a man in a blue blazer say to Esme, "Princeton? *Those* pussies? You're shitting me."

Paul slipped by, there and gone. He had two drinks in hand, and he looked at Esme, who was leaning against Jonathan, the runner, and sipping a fresh cocktail, glanced down at the drinks he was holding, one of which appeared to be for her, and handed one cocktail to another woman. The woman laughed, long crystal earrings swaying, and he touched her lightly on the back, and they disappeared into the crowd.

Esme had told Kate that Paul hoped to buy his mother a house once he finished law school, pay for her to earn a college degree. He had a younger brother, seven, whom he also hoped to send to college. Esme had said this with wonder at his nobility, at the nobility of the lower classes, and Kate had both admired his ambitions and cringed at Esme's knowing tone.

Amir, the host and heir to the hotel fortune, tapped his glass and shouted a long toast, the words of which she could not make out. An uproarious laugh greeted one comment. At the bar, a middle-aged bartender polished a wineglass and listened.

"I don't want to be here," she said on the phone.

"I'm coming to get you."

"What? No. That's crazy."

"At least tell me where you're staying."

"I don't even know."

They negotiated. He insisted he was driving to Boston that night; she said no, it would be rude and besides the snow was worsening, and finally he promised he wouldn't if she gave him the address. She found Paul, who wrote it on a cocktail napkin. Reading the address over the phone she knew it was a mistake.

"I love you," he said before they hung up. She did not reply. She believed him, but it was increasingly not enough. "Did you hear me?"

"I did."

"I'm going to drive up tomorrow. We can go to New York or Vermont, wherever you want to go. Please let me do that. I need to see you. I'm so sorry, baby, I really am."

She was tired. "Okay," she said. "I mean, let's talk about it tomorrow."

"No talking," he said. "I'm going to come."

They hung up. Esme appeared, the fine blonde hair at her temples darkened with sweat from dancing. "How are you doing?" she asked, seeing Kate standing alone, and when Kate said, "Good," Esme squeezed her arm happily in a way that signaled she'd had a lot to drink. Drinking made her more affectionate, relaxed, though no less goal oriented. Over Kate's shoulder, Esme watched Paul cross the room. The expression on her face revealed to Kate that she did, in fact, still want him but had decided to repress this feeling indefinitely. "Paul shouldn't leave you alone like this," Esme announced. "You're his *guest*." "I'm fine," Kate said. "Really, I'm having fun. I was just talking to Miriam before she went to get a drink."

"You sure?"

"Yes. How about you? Are you having fun?"

A familiar look of determination appeared on Esme's face.

"My New Year's resolution is to date one of Paul's friends," Esme cried. She pointed at a brooding guy across the room. "That one. He's a clerk for the Supreme Court."

Paul returned, alone. Paul and Kate danced. An hour and a half passed. Esme drank two more champagne cocktails, grew stumbly. The brooding guy supported her as she held court in the corner, two other men listening to her story. Kate stopped drinking and switched to water.

The night was veering out of control. A man in a red-checked shirt carried a loveseat onto the balcony, where smokers gathered and two women danced with each other sexily, touching enough that a kiss seemed at hand.

Kate lost Paul in the crowd. He'd switched to water too, though he had never seemed that drunk, and was getting them more seltzer. Esme was in the bathroom, or somewhere.

A slim girl with elegant features and Italian skin danced to the music, her drapey top swaying dangerously. The neck scooped low between her small breasts and the top was cut in a deep arc beneath her arms as well, baring an expanse of skin. She was not wearing a bra. Seeing Kate observing her, she smiled.

"How does your top stay in place?" Kate said over the music.

"I have—," the girl said, followed by a phrase Kate couldn't understand.

"I'm sorry, what?" Kate said, speaking louder.

"I said I *have*," the girl yelled, "double-stick *tape* on my *tits*."

• • •

Finding a taxi was impossible. Paul called seven cab companies, and they all said it would be two hours or more. They decided to walk. Esme was far gone enough that she did not complain. Paul helped Esme and Kate over the slippery sidewalk, one on each arm. Snow weighed down phone lines and trees, hushing the city. The storm was over, a new millennium here, and the world was blank, mute. At his apartment Esme collapsed on the futon and fell asleep.

"No," she moaned, when Paul went to lift her and carry her to bed.

"You sure?" he said. "You want to sleep here?"

"Sick," she breathed.

He brought out blankets, helped her off with her shoes and jacket. By the futon he put a bowl into which she could vomit.

Kate's head felt clear. The final whiskey had worn off. She went to get her pajamas from her suitcase and realized she'd forgotten them. "Need something?" Paul asked as she rooted around, and she confessed she had neglected to pack a nightgown. He lent her clothes to sleep in and changed into sweatpants and a T-shirt, what he'd worn when the women had arrived. She brushed her teeth first, turned out the light, and climbed into his bed. This was how things were done; they could be adult about it. There was nowhere else to sleep. Besides, the thought of sleeping next to another person was nice; after talking to Michael, she felt lonely, unsure of what to do. Paul joined her. He put an arm around her and whispered, "I wanted to kiss you all night."

"Esme would never forgive us."

"She broke up with me," he said. "We're friends, that's all. Besides, you and I have so much in common. Just ask her."

She laughed. He cupped her face in his hand and smoothed her hair from her cheek. Michael might be driving here now, she thought. On the nightstand she'd placed Esme's phone for when he called to say he was on his way. "I have a boyfriend," she said. "Kissing isn't cheating," he said. She laughed again. "Where are you from? DC? Kissing is absolutely cheating." Rolling over, she pulled away, and he sighed and lay still. "Sweet dreams," he said. "Sweet dreams," she replied. She curled around his childhood toy, a gray stuffed rabbit with a hard pink plastic nose sewn above a black embroidered mouth. Paul's self-conscious breathing evened, became the soft sound of sleep, the body taking over from the brain. On the nightstand Esme's phone was silent. Kate fell asleep waiting for it to ring.

He woke her at an hour she could not have guessed—the windowpanes were black, no warm sign of dawn tinging the darkness, so perhaps 4 or 5 a.m.?—as she dreamed she was slaloming down a run of deep, fresh powder. His body cradled hers. She felt his hand's warmth on her stomach, beneath the T-shirt she had borrowed. At first his hand exerted no pressure. Then, gently, he began to press against her stomach, shift his hand, press again a little lower, circle back, a soft, arousing palpitation. Through his boxers, two sets, really, as she had worn a spare pair to bed with his T-shirt, she could feel him growing hard.

She moved away. "I have a boyfriend," she said.

He pulled down her underwear. He took his hand and rubbed against her, feeling that she was wet, and though what he was doing felt good, she said, "We can't."

"It's okay," he told her. Before she could reply, he pushed into her, pulling up the T-shirt she wore and lightly touching her nipples with one hand as he guided himself in with the other. "That's right," he said. He began to rub her back to calm her as though she were a child. She struggled a little.

"Really," she said. "Really, we can't."

He made a shushing noise. He knows I want to, she thought.

But did she? Her body did. She did not, or was not yet convinced she did, though convincing might have been possible given time. She imagined Michael at a ski lodge in New York with his friends, talking about her dismissively. Or worse, not talking about her at all. Michael, driving here now though she had told him not to come.

A numbness set in. She felt neither panicked nor aroused. She had no decision to make; the decisions were being made for her. These men will both be successful, she thought, and perhaps they both care about me in their way. Surely, they think they do. This man, this sweet, gentle man who shared with her a single-mother upbringing and was attending Harvard Law School in order to raise himself and his family up, breathed heavily, grabbing her hip and pulling her closer. "It's okay," he murmured again. Then, more to himself than to her: "This is so good."

She would not tell Esme, she knew, and after this was over she would not bring it up with Paul, would not return his calls if he called, would avoid seeing Esme if it meant seeing him, would never see him again. And when Michael arrived the next day, flushed from the cold January air of the new year and needing to pee from the six-hour drive and angry—furious—she had slept in the bed of another man, she would weep, and she would yell at him, and she would apologize. "I couldn't reach you," she'd say. "What was I supposed to think?" She would never admit what had happened, she decided. It would only make him angrier. And if she cast it in more dramatic terms than she was willing to do, explained, emphasized, that she had said no, he would still be angry and she would be a rape victim, and that was not what she wanted to be. Those girls went around perpetually fifteen, weak, cutting themselves or wearing unattractive clothes, on the brink of crying when one didn't expect it. No thank you. She didn't want it, and what's more, she couldn't afford it. That was for people who wanted attention from the world, not people who were working to be invisible so they could rise in it, rise above their place in the only way one could: quietly, without eliciting alarm. That was for people who had given up, not for her. She would be better. She would be better than that.

Charity

I GET HOME TO Vermont from my first semester at Williams for winter break after a long, snowy ride on a Greyhound bus redolent of urine and the alcoholic tang of Wet Wipes to find my mother has had a brainstorm. She is amped up, the manic gleam of destruction in her eyes.

"I know what we'll get everyone for Christmas," she says.

She ashes her cigarette and pauses, looks at me. She is referring to her mother and three sisters, whom we mostly see on holidays. I sit patiently, trying to seem expectant. When she senses I can't take it anymore, she tells me what our gift is going to be.

"Nothing," she says.

We are sitting at the kitchen table. I am still wearing my wool coat, snow melting in the folds of the hood. Though it is five degrees outside and icicles hang from the eaves, my mother has opened the window to accommodate a fan, which faces away from us, whirring softly, blowing her smoke out of the house. I push my chair back, away from the cold air pocket by the window. My backpack hangs from my shoulder. I shrug it off, set it on the floor.

"Nothing?" I say.

"Nothing."

I look at her and wait. There's more to come, I can tell.

"They don't deserve anything," she says. "They wouldn't know what generosity was if it punched them in the face." She offers this up with a pleasure that tells me she's been turning the phrase over and over in her mind until it's acquired a high sheen.

"We can't really give them nothing," I say. "I mean, how would we wrap it?" I am kind of kidding, kind of not. For me, a lot of the joy in Christmas is in the wrapping. I love shiny stick-on bows and curling ribbons, tissue paper and cellophane, all the exuberant excess and waste.

"Well," my mother concedes, "we won't really give them nothing. What we'll do is give money to charity in their names, and then we can write it in a card."

She takes a drag on her cigarette and blows the smoke into the window fan.

"That'll teach them," she says. "That'll show them what charity is."

My mother's plan is to write in the cards that we have donated more money to charity than we really have. She doesn't want the relatives to think we're cheap.

"Fifty dollars to the poor?" I say. "When did you give fifty dollars to the poor?"

"I put some canned pineapple in the donation box at Price Chopper," she says. "You know, the Feed the Thousands one."

"Fifty dollars' worth?"

"Close enough."

This is kind of true, if you look at it like we are the poor and whatever money my mother saves on presents, she can put toward the grocery bill. Still, I don't want to sign my name to it. When my mother offers me the cards—sympathy cards from a pack of twelve she bought during the Gulf War, when she decided to write to everyone in town who was affected and realized too late she could only think of one person—I tell her she should write mine and Agnes's names in for us. But she insists we each sign our own name, and, not wanting to disappoint her, I cave.

The cards are pretty: they show a tall stand of birch, silver bark striated and stripping off. Sitting down to sign four times, I see she has taped pieces of paper with "Happy Holidays" written in green felt-tipped pen over the black script sympathy message.

"Decorative, huh?" she asks as I examine her handiwork.

"Definitely," I say. I write my name, Kate, under hers, fighting the urge to smudge the ink.

I copy out Agnes's name on a napkin, along with holiday messages she dictates to me, and she sits down to sign the four cards. Agnes is nine. Though smart, she has dysgraphia and struggles with focus. I skipped two grades; she attended prefirst, an extra one. "It takes youngest children longer," my mother always says. If forgiveness is not my mother's strong suit, Agnes is the exception that proves the rule; about Agnes, my mother interprets everything with an almost artistic disregard for the facts. When a little boy with pointy eyeteeth named Pete killed the classroom hamster by dropping it in the toilet to see whether it could swim, inspired by Agnes's assurances that this was the best way to learn, and, discovering the answer was no, rescued the poor thing too late, an accident that took place in kindergarten and left Agnes heartbroken and speaking wistfully about the fragility of life for weeks and her teacher permanently pissed, my mother said, "Agnes is an empiricist. She has a scientific mind."

Agnes is wearing a leotard, though she has stopped ballet lessons, which we could never really afford, and she taps a ballet-slippered foot against the table as she works. Her hair, pulled back in a wispy French braid, has lost the honey brown streaks it acquires at the public pool each summer. It takes her an eternity to sign the cards, what with the frequent theatrical breaks to shake out her hands, more for my mother's amusement than her own relief, but she gets it done.

"Perfect," my mother says. "Absolutely beautiful."

Agnes beams.

"Let's seal the deal," my mother says, and lets Agnes lick the gluey rims of the envelopes. She loves the taste. If you leave her alone with an envelope, she'll lick it until it's useless. She licks each envelope carefully, smacking her lips in between.

"Once'll do," my mother cautions. "If you're not careful, you're going to get a papercut on your tongue."

Agnes rolls her eyes. When my mother's back is turned, she licks the final envelope twice.

My grandfather, who was an engineer, had an explosive temper. He made my grandmother very unhappy. She treated her daughters with a coldness that transmitted this unhappiness to my mother, who remains angry with her. When my mother was fourteen, my grandfather got transferred from Michigan to an engineering lab in New Jersey, and, as a teenager, she snuck into the city, cutting school and going to the Bronx botanical gardens and getting stoned with older boys, running off to Maine as soon as she turned eighteen. She became a hippie: no religion, only love. Before I was born, she lived in an abandoned house without running water deep in the woods outside Bangor, surviving on blueberries and fresh-dug clams and whatever the boyfriend who would become my father could buy with the money he made doing odd jobs. She barely ever called home.

It's not much better now. My grandparents have divorced; they seem happier, but my mother does not. My grandmother comes in for all the blame, though I suspect she was not the worse parent, only the one more present.

"Your grandmother let a man pull out my tooth with pliers," my mother likes to say. "Without anesthetics. She had to hold me down."

I once asked my Aunt Rosemary about this. She was noncommittal. "Your mother tells it one way, my mother tells it another."

"What's Grammy's way?"

"General anesthesia was too dangerous, so the dentist gave her Novocain."

"The pliers?"

"You know," she said, swirling her hand. "One of those thingies they use at the dentist's." She made a squeezing gesture, clamping a phantom instrument. My mother snorted when I told her this. "I think I'd remember someone sticking needles in my mouth," she said. "I think I know what pliers look like."

This is just one of a list of hurts she remembers and feels acutely, one of many disappointments and sadnesses that have never lost their sting. To my way of thinking, the past is the past, and there's not much you can do about it. For my mother, though, the past is the present, its pain still sharp, and there is no comfort to be found in the months and years that go by.

Three days before Christmas, I borrow the car and take Agnes to the movies. Afterward, we get pizza and sodas at Frankie's Pizzeria, and I give her quarters to play the arcade games. She loves the racing game and plays until she gets nauseous.

While we wait for Agnes's stomach to settle, I buy her a ginger ale. She sips it and breathes heavily through her mouth. Then she says she feels better, and we drive across town to Ames to do our shopping. The store has been in bankruptcy proceedings for months, so it always has good sales.

We are getting presents for the relatives, I have decided. My mother can't really have meant that Agnes and I weren't to buy them anything ourselves, could she? Of course she could; I know this, but I choose to believe otherwise because it would be too embarrassing to show up empty-handed. We pool our money: the hundred dollars I've saved from my work-study job in the lab, the twenty dollars my mother has given Agnes to buy me a present. We agree the presents will be from us both. Agnes hands over her share, all in rumpled ones. Then she asks for ten dollars back.

Agnes has an eye for the gaudy and the plentiful. She makes a case for buying everyone a ham-sized set of pink and purple seashell-shaped soaps packed in shrink-wrapped baskets of wood shavings. They reek of cheap perfume. She also likes cheap gold-plated charms shaped like angels.

"Snazzy," Agnes says. It is her new favorite word. She holds a charm up to the fluorescent lights and the gold glitters.

I talk her into a compromise position: one thing each person might actually want, and the gold charms.

Picking out the other presents, I total the cost in my head, including tax, and when we pay, I am happy to find my math confirmed by the register. I have thirty dollars left, what I need to buy Agnes the Lego castle set she wants. "It's got turrets," my mother wrote on the list she transcribed.

But then, on our way out, a pair of earrings in the jewelry display case catches Agnes's attention.

"Wait," she says.

I have already walked through the security sensors, triggering the store alarm, which has just finished sounding. I walk back through to get Agnes, sounding the alarm again. The cashier glares at me, as though I've shoplifted and returned in order to make her do extra work. I shrug at her and join Agnes at the glass case.

"Those ones," she says, pointing to a set of earrings on the display case's top shelf. I crouch next to her. The earrings are shaped like elephants. Each elephant hangs in three pieces on a wire loop: in front, the head with its thick curved trunk; then the front half of the body, a heavy circle with two fat legs; then the back half, with the other two legs and a little tail poking off to the side. The saleswoman lifts the rack from the case, the hoops sway, and the elephants seem to walk.

Up close, you can see the detailing. Agnes points out the wrinkles carved into the elephants' trunks, how the ends are notched. "Like real elephants," she assures me, as though biological accuracy were the hallmark of a quality earring. She points out that elephants are our mother's favorite—news to me, but quite possibly true—and that we have thirty dollars left. She points out that it's Christmas.

I ask the saleswoman how much.

"Twenty-five," she says. "Plus tax."

I tell Agnes that I haven't done her shopping yet. They are nice elephants, but maybe next year. She gives me a look that says next year is bullshit. Okay, I say, maybe Mother's Day.

"Thanks for showing us," I tell the woman. She puts the earrings back in the display case, setting them swaying again.

Agnes stands there, chewing her lip.

"You could use my money," she says, tentatively. She means the thirty dollars.

"Then I wouldn't have a present for you, goose," I say.

We leave the store. The alarm wails.

We're almost to the car when Agnes says, "I want to go back."

"Back where?" I ask.

"To get the elephants."

I am cold and want to be in the heated car. I open the door.

"Hop in," I say to Agnes. She stands in the middle of the parking lot. Her nose is reddened and wind-chapped. Her long brown hair, done in two pigtails, peeks from under her pink wool hat. "We'll discuss this inside."

"Use my thirty dollars," she says. "Other people will get me presents."

"Agnes, that's sweet, but, really, we can't," I say. "Mom wouldn't be happy if she knew." This is true. She loves Agnes with a breathtaking ferocity. "What if we return the bird feeder we got her and buy the earrings instead?"

"No," she says. This time it's with conviction. "I want the elephants to be my present."

So we buy them. At my request, the saleswoman puts them in a black velvet case for us, even though they usually come in a plain white box. Agnes strokes the velvet as I hand over the rest of our money.

On the way home, though she cannot possibly believe this anymore, Agnes says under her breath, as if reassuring herself she's made the right decision, "Santa always brings the things I really want."

What bothers my mother about her family, she says, isn't that they have more money than we do and look down on us. It's that they are greedy. Every year, Aunt Rosemary asks for an expensive German-made bread knife. Why she hasn't bought it herself is a mystery; she loves to shop, and she spends a ton on seasonal decor, which my mother finds ridiculous. She hasn't, though, and each year, she asks again. "I can hope, can't I?" she says.

Having called to arrange plans for Christmas dinner, which we eat at Aunt Rosemary's house, my mother hangs up and says, "That goddamn bread knife. She brought it up again."

I remind my mother that Rosemary includes inexpensive items on her list too: kitchen gadgets, cheap gloves, paperback mysteries with identical breathless blurbs.

"Yes," my mother says, "but we all know she doesn't really want them."

The rest of the family is, in my mother's view, no better. Aunt Clare is rich, or what we consider rich, with her consultant husband and nice house in Massachusetts, which automatically makes her greedy. Aunt Ivy, a middle-school teacher, is friends with Rosemary and Clare, which makes her guilty by association. In my mother's mind, my grandmother is greedy too, but more subtle about it. Every year, she insists that she doesn't want anything for Christmas, and every year my mother says, "This year, she just might get it." My mother thinks her mother's self-renunciation is a greediness for piety, for superiority. It is a rebuke of my mother's desires, small though they are, a rebuke of the very act of having them. It makes her furious.

I am not sure what upsets my mother more: when people want things from her, or when they don't.

"What should Grammy do?" I ask. "Make up things she wants?"

"Noooo," my mother says, considering.

"Maybe she really doesn't want anything."

"Maybe."

"So why should she pretend to?"

"It's not *what* she says, exactly," she concludes. "It's more the *way* she says it."

The day before Christmas, I go back to Ames and use my credit card to charge the Lego set with the turrets. I have only used the credit card—really my mother's, which has a five hundred dollar limit and is only for emergencies, and which I pay off myself—two times: once to buy a bus ticket home, and once when my paycheck was delayed because of a clerical error in the college payroll office and I worked late at the lab and missed dinner and had to buy a meal. I don't like owing money. I'd rather go without than charge. But this is for Agnes. I hand the card to the cashier and tell myself it's the American way, that it is, in fact, anti-American *not* to go into debt for Christmas.

Christmas Eve, after Agnes has gone to bed, I show my mother the Lego set.

"Oh, good. It's the one with turrets," she says, examining the box.

I help her wrap Agnes's presents. She sorts them into Santa presents and Mom presents, reserving the best for Santa, including a little pistol that lights up and makes an ack-ack-ack noise when you press the plastic trigger. It sounds to me like a cat choking on a hairball.

"I thought you said no guns?"

"I did. Then her best friend got one. The school play was about Bonny and Clyde, and they're obsessed."

Agnes is a funny mix of feminine and tomboy. My mother doesn't want her to grow out of this, to grow up. She looks nostalgic as she wraps. The presents are numerous; she has, as usual, gone overboard. It takes us an hour. We use special wrapping paper for the Santa presents—blue, with embossed white snowflakes—and my mom writes those gift tags with her left hand.

"When are you going to tell her about Santa?" I ask. "I mean, she's nine. The other kids in her class definitely know."

"Pass me the clear tape," she says. She anchors a small, already wrapped present—batteries, the size suggests—to a bigger one so the boxes resemble a wedding cake. "You believed until you were nine."

I remember knowing when I was seven and pretending to believe for several more years to make her happy, and wonder if Agnes is doing the same. The world loves a little girl's innocence, her trust; she surely senses this. But I think of her reassuring herself in the car. The moment seemed too guileless to have been faked. Of course, this might be a false dialectic. Maybe she doesn't think of it as faking. Maybe pretending to believe is, to her, a different kind of truth.

Christmas morning, Agnes wakes us at dawn. In the early morning darkness, the tree's fragrant green branches glitter with ornaments, strings of lights blinking on and off through the tinsel, casting a warm glow on the presents beneath. Outside, the rising sun glimmers pink on our snowy front yard, ice-coated pine needles bright and glasslike. We admire the sight, and my mother goes into the kitchen to heat oil for fried dough. We aren't allowed to open presents until we've eaten, but Agnes kneels, checking name tags, shaking boxes. She smells a few for good measure.

After breakfast, we open our presents. Agnes loves the Legos and the pistol that makes the hairball noise. My mother loves the bird feeder. I love the cashmere blend sweater my mother has bought me, a gray crewneck like the ones my classmates at Williams wear, and pretend to love Agnes's present, a unicorn pin with fake inlaid jewels, which I plan to return after wearing once.

We finish, and I realize the elephant earrings are missing. I feel a moment of panic, and then Agnes says, "And now for the grand finale."

She runs upstairs, taking the stairs fast, and comes back down with a box she's wrapped herself. The paper's corners, folded into chunky triangles, strain against the Scotch tape. To compensate, she has run many loops around the box like see-through ribbon. My mother disentangles the box from the tape while Agnes stands, poised with the disposable camera.

My mother flips open the black velvet case. When she sees the elephants, she grins, just positively glows. The hooks are sunk into cotton padding—the case is meant for brooches—and she pulls them out carefully, setting the case on the couch's arm. She holds up the earrings like she's caught a fish and Agnes snaps a picture. She hugs us both and puts them in her ears.

The phone rings and Agnes goes to answer it.

"Hello," she says into the cordless phone. "And a merry Christmas to you."

"She said elephants were your favorite," I say.

My mother laughs. "They're *her* favorite," she says. "She likes the idea that they have elaborate burial rituals for their dead. The herd revisits the burial sites every year. They can find the bones even after they've trekked a hundred miles away and back."

"That's pretty amazing," I say.

My mother shrugs. "I find it kind of creepy. That, and their trunks."

Though my mother usually makes fun of women who wear dresses in the winter, when we get ready to go to Aunt Rosemary's for dinner, she changes from her sweatshirt and sweatpants into a long red flower-print shift.

"A dress?" I say.

"I want to look nice."

"For the relatives?"

"No," she says, pulling on snow boots. "Who cares what those people think? For myself."

Her hair has tangled in the elephant earrings. She tries to pull it loose, winces, and I go to help her.

Agnes slides across the floor in her socks, holding her pistol with both hands, stops in front of us, and takes aim. She shoots me, and I wait for the ack-ack-ack noise to stop before I resume freeing the elephants.

"Agnes, we discussed this," my mother says. "Not at people."

"Then what am I supposed to shoot?"

"Things," my mother says, making a general, expansive motion with her hand.

"You look beautiful, Mom," Agnes says. Then she shoots her.

"Agnes!"

"You gave it to her," I say.

Agnes shoots her again.

"The gift that keeps on giving," my mother says.

Before we leave, my mother tucks the cards into her purse. I go upstairs and, with a sense of misgiving, load the presents Agnes and I bought into my backpack.

When we pull up to Aunt Rosemary's house, the windows are ablaze with Christmas lights though it's daytime. A gigantic plastic light-up snowman glows brightly on the lawn like the radioactive survivor of a world war.

"Here we go," my mother says.

Aunt Rosemary greets us at the door. She is wearing a green-and-red sweater with gold pom-poms.

"Merry Christmas," she says. She gives my mother a smile and nod and me a friendly one-armed hug. Then she goes to hug Agnes, but Agnes is reaching to touch the tiny ring of pom-poms on Aunt Rosemary's sleeve, so instead, Aunt Rosemary holds out her wrist as though offering her hand to be kissed.

Agnes takes her hand and turns it to examine the pom-poms. "Snazzy," she pronounces.

"Macy's was having a sale," Aunt Rosemary says. "It was half off."

I hear a snort behind me. I hope silently that my mother won't say anything. I look over my shoulder, and she smiles at me in a conspiratorial way. Aunt Rosemary has already stepped inside and is saying, "Come in, it's freezing out there."

In the kitchen, Aunt Ivy is taking the turkey out of the oven. "Come in, come in!" she calls. "Dinner's almost ready."

Despite her recently renovated kitchen, Rosemary doesn't cook. She's more of a microwaver. Ivy, the family peacemaker and a sixth-grade teacher used to tolerating outbursts, handles holiday meals, offering food or retreating into chores when tensions rise.

"Smells good," I say.

"Rosemary's doing the sides this year," Ivy says. She means it as praise, but it sounds like a warning.

My grandmother hobbles over to us, dressed, as usual, in a matching powder blue nylon pantsuit, hair permed in tight, sensible spirals, looking trim and no-nonsense. She has started using a cane since I saw her last. She gives me a hug and then goes for my mother. My mother avoids the hug, pats her shoulder gingerly.

While my mother is occupied, I sneak into the living room and put Agnes's and my presents under the tree. "Better to ask forgiveness than permission," my tenth-grade history teacher used to say, "or so Nixon believed." Agnes lives her life by it.

The gifts here are few. I've wrapped our boxes in plain red foil paper, but the other presents are wrapped in green tissue paper, so ours shine like roadside flares. Seeing them, conspicuous and exposed, I begin to lose my nerve. Maybe I should put the gifts back in my backpack, hide them until we've said our goodbyes and then duck into the house and leave them with the relatives? But Agnes is sure to ask if I've forgotten them, unless I can get her alone and explain. And what will I say? I can't justify my mother's logic to myself, let alone to Agnes. I stand by the tree, debating, until my mother walks in.

"There you are," she says.

I steer her into the dining room.

Aunt Rosemary has set the Christmas china. This year, there's a new addition: bronze napkin rings shaped like reindeer. They stand on duty by the plates, legs planted solidly on the wood, antlers rising skyward, middles run through with red and green cloth napkins. It occurs to me that Aunt Rosemary is wearing camouflage; if things get ugly, she can hold still and she'll blend right in.

Agnes fingers an antler.

"Aunty Rosemary," she calls to the kitchen, where Aunt Rosemary is scooping mashed potatoes into a bowl held by Aunt Ivy, "when you die, can I have your Christmas plates?"

"What?" she calls back.

"She says she likes the reindeer," I call.

Before eating, we hold hands and bow our heads while my grandmother says grace. Agnes and I pretend, like we always do. My mother keeps her eyes open.

Dinner is quiet. No one knows what to say. It is like dinner with strangers, but more treacherous. We pass the serving dishes efficiently, a line of sandbaggers moving to stanch a leak. The green beans are the frozen kind, and the cranberry sauce is still shaped like the can it came from. We eat fast.

"I wish Clare and the boys could be here," my grandmother says, as she does every year. Aunt Clare is skiing in Colorado with her family. My grandmother doesn't like Clare's husband, so he doesn't get mentioned. Her way is to ignore what she doesn't like.

"I don't," my mother says. The table goes quiet. "Well, I don't."

"Could you pass the green beans?" my grandmother asks.

"Clare dropped my kids the second she had her own," my mother says. "She was Kate's favorite aunt. Kate was crushed. Now Clare can't be bothered to remember their birthdays. She and Tom don't even get us presents for Christmas, they just send whatever free crap is lying around the house." This is, in fact, the case—during the holidays, they wrap up product samples from whatever company Tom is consulting for and give them to my grandmother to bring to us—but we aren't supposed to say so.

"That's enough," my grandmother says.

"No, I don't think it is," my mother says, but she leaves it at that.

Five Christmases ago, my mother baked bread as our family gift. That was a bad year, our first welfare year. We didn't have cash, but we had food stamps. My mother looked up recipes for zucchini bread. She grew the zucchini herself in her vegetable garden out behind our house, deer-besieged but capable of producing more tomatoes and peas and squash each summer than we could eat. She spent a whole weekend baking. She compared recipes, trying three ways before settling on the best. Once the bread was done, she asked me to make the loaves pretty. I wrapped them in colored cellophane and tied the ends with ribbon. Agnes helped me make cards out of scraps of wrapping paper.

Examining her package, Aunt Rosemary had announced, "I'm on a diet."

"Clare's been making wheat germ bread," my grandmother said. "She's got me eating it now."

"But you like zucchini bread too," my mother said.

"Oh, I do," said my grandmother. "It's delicious. I just don't eat it anymore."

Aunt Ivy, ever the peacemaker, said, "Well, then, I'll eat both of yours." But she only took her own when she left.

A few days later, we stopped by Aunt Rosemary's to return the two Tupperware containers we'd borrowed for leftovers. She was outside on her lawn, feeding the zucchini bread to a flock of birds. My mother slowed down, took in the scene, and then sped up. She said she'd remembered an errand she had to do at Price Chopper. When we got to the supermarket, she said, "Wait here. It'll only take a minute." Then she walked over to the big trashcan outside the automated doors and threw away the Tupperware.

· · ·

After we eat, we troop into the living room to open presents. My grandmother moves slowly in the direction of my mother, who, seeing her coming, darts into the bathroom to avoid her. Turning to me, my grandmother pats my arm affectionately. Then her fingers dig into my skin and she leans in and I realize that without her cane, she needs me to hold her up. She is shorter than me and frail, too small, it would seem, for the weight on my arm. I help her to the couch, and she says, "Now, where did your mother go?"

"Not sure," I mumble.

Aunt Rosemary and Aunt Ivy herd Agnes into an easy chair. She is fidgety with anxiety and caffeine, having been allowed a milky cup of Earl Grey tea. She raises and lowers the footrest, repeats this maneuver until Aunt Ivy asks her to stop. My mother comes in, having pretended to use the bathroom for a reasonable length of time. She carries her purse, cards tucked inside. Catching my eye, she grins at me, excited for our big moment.

Aunt Rosemary sits near the tree and hands out packages, reading the gift tags aloud. She always buys me and Agnes identical presents. This year, we both receive clock radios. She keeps passing over the presents Agnes and I have bought.

Then Aunt Rosemary says, "Oh, look—from Agnes and Kate."

My mother gives me a quick, sharp look. I shrug as innocently as I can manage. The joy is gone from her face. I see in her expression what I knew all along: what was important about giving our relatives nothing was that we do it together. As a family. I feel a queasiness that isn't located in my stomach, but my heart.

"That was nice of you," my mother says to me. She means it, I can tell, but she is also hurt and struggling to hide it.

"What?" Aunt Rosemary says.

"Nothing," she says.

As everybody opens our presents, my mother looks down. No one else seems to notice. They thank us, and Agnes looks pleased. I want to apologize to my mother, but I don't know how.

"We forgot to write that our presents are from Mom, too," I say. "On the tags." I look at Agnes as I speak so she'll catch on. "Remember, Mom? We talked about it?"

"No," my mother says. "You and Agnes picked those out. Those were just from you."

My grandmother has her own cards, which she hands around. The aunts, Agnes, and I each receive a gift certificate for twenty dollars.

My mother does not receive a gift certificate. In my mother's card is a check.

She stares at it, stunned. She doesn't say anything. Everyone waits, and finally Rosemary says, "What is it?" but my mother doesn't answer. I scootch next to her on the couch, look over her shoulder. The check is for twelve thousand dollars.

"I'm not getting any younger," my grandmother says. "It's important to plan ahead. I'm going to rotate between you kids from year to year. That's—" she nods at the check—"the per person cap."

"I can't take this," my mother says. Her hands tremble a little as she tries to give my grandmother back the check.

"Oh, honey, don't be silly," my grandmother says.

"I don't want your money."

"And I don't want your excuses."

My mother shrugs. She puts the check in her purse. She is shaken, her mouth drawn, on the verge of tears.

Beneath the tree, no more packages remain. My mother looks around the room at each of us, torn gift wrap at our feet, presents in our laps. She examines the tree for a minute. Then, slowly, she takes the cards from her purse and hands them around.

My grandmother is the first to read her card.

"Well," she says, "that is very generous."

Aunt Rosemary and Aunt Ivy open their cards.

"I was hoping for a bread knife," Aunt Rosemary says. She laughs in a way that says she isn't kidding, but her laugh is more bemused than covetous. "But this is very nice."

"Thank you," Aunt Ivy says. "What charity did you give to?"

"Feed the Thousands," my mother says.

"Very generous," my grandmother repeats. "How nice that you can give back, after that tough time you had."

My mother flinches. Then she looks down at her lap and nods privately, as though something's been confirmed. We all sit quietly. Finally, my mother pulls a pack of cigarettes from her purse. She waves them at us and says, "I'll be outside."

"Oh, dear," my grandmother says to me after my mother closes the door. We can see her through the window, standing on the steps, lighting up. The sky is gray. "Your mother always was a sensitive girl. Whatever I say, it's never enough for her. Whatever I do, it will never be enough."

We have coffee, but still my mother doesn't come in. After twenty minutes, I go to get her for dessert and find her under the maple tree on the edge of my aunt's lawn, sitting in the tire swing, smoking her fifth or sixth cigarette. The snow is packed down and dirty. Butts litter the area by her feet. She has put on a coat, but it doesn't cover her legs. Her bare calves are goose pimpled and white.

"That woman," she says. "She always finds a way."

I don't know exactly what she means, but I know it's not good. I search for something to say, something ambiguous.

She gets out of the tire swing and kicks at the snow with her boot, scattering it over the butts. I take her place on the tire, push the swing back and forth with my feet and look up at her. She waits.

"She loves you," I say.

"She's got a funny way of showing it," my mother says. "Couldn't she just once say *thank you* and mean it?"

"She could," I say. "But then what would you hate her for?" I regret saying it as soon as I've spoken, but my mother laughs.

"Oh, I'd find something," she says.

I look at my mother's bare legs, and I think, the past is a place I'm glad I don't live.

"That money," I say. "It's your inheritance. You're just getting it early. You should keep it."

"Maybe," says my mother. "Maybe I will. I guess I will."

The wind picks up. The snow is granular, little needles stinging my face. My mother clutches the neck of her coat. The bottom of her dress blows up and she clamps it between her knees.

I climb off the swing. "Inside?" I say.

"Oh, hell. I guess so," she says.

The path to the house is frozen and slippery. My mother has on her snow boots, but I am wearing regular shoes, and walking toward the house, I almost fall. My mother tucks her arm through mine, and we pick our way across the icy lawn. The giant plastic snowman bows in a gust of wind, casts his glow across the snow.

The house looks deserted. Aunt Ivy is, I'm sure, serving dessert, as if a little sweetness can undo all the bitterness and pain, make our hearts swell like the Grinch's until they burst the magnifying glass. My mother tries the knob. The door is locked. The wind whips our hair in our faces, the snowman bobbing crazily toward us, reversing direction as the wind changes. We knock and wait, blowing on our hands and stomping our feet. Then we knock again.

The Foothills of Tucson

CITY LIGHTS SPREAD below, shimmering and pulsing and rippling like water. Behind, the dark hills hung with dark sky. Stars scattered bright as polished bone. I don't know the name for the color of night here. It's like skin: the color changes as it thins. Near the city, a translucent faded black lit from within by a pinkish gray bulb. Where it touches the hills, a deep blue. Only in the middle does it approach—but never becomes—true black. And the moon. I knew the sun would be intense, but I wasn't prepared for this moon. It's not cold and distant, like the moon in the eastern sky. This moon is big and close. The light it gives off is like a headlight.

I used to think Tucson was ugly. Flying in at 3 a.m., hurtling through the desert in a cab, religious billboards looming over scrubby vegetation: not the best first impression. One billboard was all black, with white letters that read, "One nation under me. —God." I wanted to tell the cab driver to turn around, take me back to the airport, book a flight to Boston. Or to drive straight through, and I'd sleep the whole way east. Now, I don't even notice the billboards. Andy was visiting in March, and he pointed one out. I had to look up to see what he meant.

I wish you could see this. Not just Tucson, but the whole Southwest—the place I've lived these past two years, until recently a foreign place, which still startles me with its beauty and hostility but no longer its unfamiliarity. Meaning it's become a part of me. Meaning I've become a foreign place.

Andy asked about you. I told him I supposed you were fine.

I like my life here. I live alone, in a tiny guesthouse. Jewel box–sized. The front room is brick floored with a slanted roof, and the white stucco wall outside is overgrown with vines. A tangle of leaves, waxy and dense. I like looking out the windows at the green, a tiny glowing bit of blue sky. I cook Spanish tortilla on the antique white stove and eat it with a wedge of Manchego and a chilled tomato salad. When friends visit, we sit on facing couches and use an old wooden chest for our plates. There isn't room for a proper kitchen table. Most days, I eat outside, on the narrow patio.

You'd like this life too, I think. It's something I'd like to show you. To hold up and say, look what I've built.

The panic I felt when you said we had to separate: I think it was in part because I'd never seen a life I would want before I met you, and I didn't believe I could make a life like that—like yours—for myself. But it wasn't just that. I know that now, when so many days you are the only person I want to talk to. I call friends, go through four or five, before I know for sure.

The optical sciences program here is good, better than you'd expect. I was surprised myself, when I began asking around. So is the astronomy program. The Steward Observatory is excellent. Harvard scientists come here to do research. But national reputations aren't built on graduate programs, I suppose. I tell people back East where I go to school, and a look of confusion overtakes them, and then they say brightly, "Oh, right, that online school." They think I mean the University of Phoenix. I used to try to explain. Now I just nod.

When I began researching graduate programs, that I could leave New England—that I could leave you—hadn't even occurred to me. Then Dr. Paulson saying, "No, no, for what you want to do, the University of Arizona is the place," scribbling the email address of a professor to contact, one of his old grad school friends. The thrill, and the pain, when I realized I could go so far away, that staying in Cambridge, near you, would be a choice.

Mailing my application to Arizona felt impetuous. Crazy, even. We were already through, but I counted on our chance meetings. You did too, I think. I guess we were both hoping life would throw us together again. But that only happens in movies. That it happened the first time was already a miracle.

Two years, and another three or four to go, depending on my research, unless I decide to leave the PhD program and go into industry, which I don't think I will. Every month, the department chair forwards emails to the graduate listserv for jobs that pay more money than I ever imagined making. I guess I could apply, move to a different city, get a nice car, maybe a house. Buy myself some security. But that's not why I came.

Yesterday was September twenty-third, the first day of autumn. I woke homesick for New England. The smell of wool sweaters shaken out after being stored for summer. Mulled apple cider chalked on the menu of local cafes. The gray pall of the sky that casts a net over you, delicate and chilling. The slight melancholy the fading of summer brings—a sense that to live is to die a little, day by day, but that it's an okay trade. Here, autumn just means I can run in the late afternoons instead of waiting for the coolness of dark.

Later, on campus, emerging from the gloom of the windowless laboratory, the feeling came back, but stronger. The world of the laboratory always looks the same, with its electric lighting, seen through protective glasses that guard against laser reflections, and the sunlit world outside looked the same as it always did too, no indication that September was any different from June, and I had the distinct sense that my life wasn't passing. I went into Harvill's third-floor women's bathroom, which reminds me of a high school gym bathroom, with its opaque high windows bolted shut and tilt-anchored stainless-steel mirrors that always make the person reflected look dim, ghostly, because of their positioning. For a minute, it was hard to breathe. The past seemed so far away and so near, and I was hit with this vertigo, like I was falling out of myself. I splashed water on my face and went out into the sunshine and sat on the low cement wall by the bike racks, ate a bean burrito wrapped in tinfoil by the cheerful Russian girl who works the taco stand. I wasn't really hungry. I bought it to prove to myself that my life here was real. When I walked up the girl said, "The usual?" I was so thankful I put a five-dollar bill in her Styrofoam tip cup. She's saving for college, I heard her say once.

I look at the Russian girl sometimes and think about what I'd tell her if I knew her beyond overhearing what she says to her coworkers about her life while I wait for my change. Meaning, of course, what I wish someone had told me ten years ago, when I was sixteen. Maybe that sometimes it's as important to travel away from what you want as it is to travel toward it. Or maybe nothing. Maybe there's nothing you can say.

I was twenty-four when I moved here. With the exception of a few months in California, I'd barely been outside the Northeast. In Tucson, it was monsoon season—August, a week before the graduate college orientation. The radio was full of warnings about the heat. My apartment was unfurnished and empty; I'd sold my furniture in Boston, brought only a suitcase of clothes. That first night, I slept on a half-deflated air mattress. When I rolled over, my elbow or hip concentrating pressure, the rubber sagged in response and I felt the wood floor. The next day, the temperature broke 110. A wind storm kicked up dust and gave me a face full of grit every time I stepped outside. The hot air felt like a blast from a high-powered hair dryer. I've never felt more alone.

Funny to remember first hearing your voice on my voicemail. The gray light of a Boston winter late afternoon. I'd just driven three hundred miles through a blizzard, from upstate New York, those towns with cramped, mildewed names—Binghamton, Elmira, Alfred—to Massachusetts, a drive that should've taken four hours accordioned by sleet. Seven hours of staring at the slushy, treacherous highway, passing accident after accident, sand trucks blinking ahead, yellow and red lights little beacons as I crept along at thirty-five, forty. Seven hours in a silent gray-white fog. Why had I gone into the lab? It was four-thirty, an hour before the end of the workday, not enough time to accomplish anything real, just check email and listen to my voicemails. Which is what I did. And there, between colleagues, your voice, unexpected, a little sheepish, a little something else. I wasn't sure what.

I knew who you were right away, even before you said your name. Your voice was enough. It bridged the two weeks between that day and the lab's annual holiday party, where you'd waited on us, running from dining room to kitchen to fetch wine, extra limes, seltzer for spills, while we mingled and got drunk. After dinner, lingering while a friend got her coat, I apologized to you for our principal investigator's bad behavior—he'd snapped his fingers when he wanted another drink, like he was calling a dog—and we began talking, the kind of conversation two people have when they're drawn to each other but know they'll probably never talk again. I told you about how I'd become interested in science, which was, for me, a way of asking questions of the world, and you told me you were a painter, a lecturer at the Museum School, working the occasional private party at the restaurant for cash. I leaned into your voice, low, wry, the first thing I loved about you. We talked about Cezanne, whom we both loved, and Morandi, whom you loved and I did not. All those murky, diminutive forms. You had a gap between your front teeth—on you it was appealing, and I could see why people say it's good luck—and curly hair, which I'd never found especially attractive before and surprised myself by liking. When I left, you held out your hand and said your name, and I told you mine, and that would have been that had you not later checked the restaurant's reservation log, called information for my lab's number, asked for me. New Year's Eve, and I was out, of course, as you'd surely guessed I would be, but it must have seemed symbolic, an auspicious time to commit to changing your future. Like making a resolution. You left your school office number on the message. You didn't say that was what it was—I found out later.

I almost didn't call you. I was still involved with my college boyfriend, who was at Cornell, and I was not the kind of person who would cheat on her boyfriend, even at that age. I'm still not sure why I picked up the phone. Maybe it was the blizzard, the surreal cottony feeling staring at hundreds of miles of snow had induced in me. A sense I was somehow insulated. Or seeing so many cars off the road. I didn't know then that you were living with someone. If I'd known, I'm almost certain I wouldn't have called.

Later, I figured it out: rueful. Your voice was a little rueful.

I went to a club last night. My friend Sylvie invited me. She's in the English program, which is mostly single women, and they're always trying to meet guys. Level, the club's name was, a chichi place on River and Campbell in an upscale shopping development that a year ago I would've called a strip mall and located by neighborhood rather than cross street. I talked with a guy about the war. Or rather, he talked with me. He told me that even if eighty percent of the Muslim population were moderate, twenty percent is still a lot of people who want to destroy America. We have every right to invade solemn nations if their leaders say they'd use weapons of mass destruction against us, he went on. He was kind of spitting as he talked. I argued with him and finally, tired and disgusted and having gotten nowhere, turned away. But I kept thinking, Sovereign. You mean sovereign nations. I thought of the time you meant to say "Scandinavian" and you said "Scandivian" instead and, realizing your mistake, began an impromptu lecture about the Scandivians. "Now, the Scandivians are a strange people. A people who live mostly underground in hollowed-out dens. A people drawn to the tambourine." I don't know what made it so funny. Probably the glee on your face. That and the PBS tone your voice adopted, the slightly nasal quality.

Some days, I still think I need you. I want to make blueberry buckwheat waffles like the ones you made on rainy Saturday mornings and I don't know how, and I pick up the phone and dial the first four digits of your number. But then I remind myself I can look up a recipe, and if it isn't the right one, well, I can try again. That such things aren't exclusively your domain.

Of course, the real reason I think I need you isn't waffles. I remind myself of that too.

Strange to think the desert is where I passed the mark from girlhood to adulthood. I wonder what did it. Not a birthday, though my last—twenty-six—felt significant. Not a sexual experience. Nothing like that. Not something done to my body, by time or by another person. Something less discrete. Something invisible, accretive.

You'd recognize me, of course, if you saw me. I still look the same, if a little tanner, a little older. I cut my hair short, too. This is the desert, after all. But it wouldn't be the physical differences that would remind you how long we've been apart. Or at least, it's not the physical differences that remind me.

If I'd known how I'd come to feel about you and that we'd only have two years together, not a whole lifetime, I wonder if I would've kissed you sooner. I think I would have. But you were still living with your girlfriend, and I clung to a belief that if we did everything *right*, we'd be rewarded. Now, I wonder, by whom? And what line exactly did I think kissing would cross that falling in love hadn't?

That night in April when you tried, both of us a little drunk, I don't think you understood why I turned my head. You thought I was upset, maybe even angry with you, but that wasn't it. It was an attempt to safeguard what I felt in my chest: a line between us, invisible but taut, unbreakable as fishing line. When your lips grazed my jawbone below my ear, I smelled the odor of spike lavender on your skin, herbaceous and faintly sweet, an alternative to mineral spirits with their aromatic hydrocarbons, the smell of which you disliked more, and I thought of how you'd climb into bed beside your girlfriend later and that smell would be so familiar to her that she might not even notice it, and then whatever that line was anchored to inside me gave a little, and I felt as though you and I would never be together. Thinking of that woman I'd never met and only half-believed in waiting for you, I couldn't imagine anything, even a real kiss, even sex, erasing the space between us. That terrible sinking sensation you get when an elevator drops too fast, when you think you're one place and then your body realizes you're another: that was it. The feeling faded, of course, but it never left me. Not completely.

The next day—the same day, really, we'd been out so late—you called the lab and said you had to see me. You biked across the city, from Huntington to Kendall Square, through the traffic lights that stud Mass Ave, and I invented an errand and met you in the little corporate park behind our office. The building's high aluminum façade cast a shadow over the grass, darkening the new green shoots to the color of old blown glass. It had rained that morning, and the air was a little nippy, but headed toward warm.

As I waited for you, I leaned against an oak tree, then walked around it, tapping acorns into the soft earth and getting my shoes muddy. My long wool skirt hobbled me, forced me to take small steps, and when you biked up in your torn, paint-stained khakis, fisherman's sweater unraveling at the sleeve, face flushed from the exertion and the cold sea air that blows across the Mass Ave bridge, I envied you your freedom. And then you saw me and smiled, and I envied myself, if such a thing is possible.

You swung off your bike and leaned it against the iron railing. Until that afternoon, we'd always met at night, after you'd gotten off a restaurant shift or spent a late evening painting in your faculty studio in the Museum School's basement. Seeing your face in daylight, I realized the sixteen years between us. I'd known, of course, but the knowledge had felt abstract. But there was nothing abstract about you in the park, sunlight picking up the red in your beard's stubble that was gone from your hair. The sun shadowed the papery lines that fanned from your eyes, precise but soft, like a Japanese ink wash painting. As though your skin was water, dissolving what time sketched. I remember the shock of seeing your future superimposed on your face. Though of course it wasn't your future—the illusion worked the other way around. I was just coming to recognize the present.

We fell into step, you wheeling your bicycle between us, the happiness dropping away from your face. You apologizing, apologizing, me thinking I'd ruined everything.

After that, silence. I'd broken up with my boyfriend, and I thought I'd lost you too, even your friendship, which was all I'd really had, and I was beginning to reconcile myself to being alone, until, two months later, you called to say you'd moved out, and could I please meet you right away, that night?

My research team just found out that we've been awarded a major grant. It's good news because of the money and because it means that the grant agency thinks the work we're doing is viable. So much of science is investigating dead ends.

I used to wait for events like this, thinking they'd be what made me happy. Even when the moments arrived, though, they didn't feel like the real thing. You were never that way; you acted on your impulses. You weren't irresponsible, but you were a bit of a hedonist. You didn't seem to trust the future. It was like you looked ahead and saw darkness and said, Fuck it. I'm going to have what I can have now. And maybe you were right. I'm beginning to suspect so. I'm trying to let myself give in a little more.

You were funny about pleasure, though, because for all your abandon, you seemed to need to punish yourself. That sadness you carried around, you hid it well, but not so well I couldn't see it. It crept into your face when you were tired. You told me once about your gentle mother, who died when you were my age, the cassette tape she recorded for you of herself singing and playing the piano. She made it when she knew she would die soon; she wanted you to have it, a comfort. You never listened. As far as I know, you still haven't. I sometimes felt that you thought you needed sadness to define yourself, that some part of you wanted to be lonely. And your work—it was never about sensual pleasure, though you loved Rothko, those fields of color as dazzling and comforting as a real field made of grass and earth. As purifying.

Today, at Albertsons, I wanted flowers. I bought yellow snapdragons. At home, I didn't have vases, so I used three empty mineral water bottles—each bottle held two stems. The green bottles and yellow flowers, lined up, looked so pretty. If you painted them, I suppose you'd paint them gray, drain the color to emphasize form or the viewer's expectations, but it would be a mistake. Or maybe the mistake would be painting them in the first place. Art isn't about prettiness, I know, but the world needs some prettiness. Some things should be allowed that.

I've started dating a guy here, a postdoc at the observatory named Javier. I don't love him, but he's kind, we like the same movies, it's easy to spend time with him. Is that enough? Probably not, but maybe for now. He's nothing like you, and I guess that's a relief. I should like him more: he's twenty-six too, smart, funny, and he wants me to be his girlfriend. He wants to take me to parties and introduce me to his friends, to go away for the weekend, stay at bed and breakfasts together, go on hikes. All the usual stuff two people do when they think they might be falling in love. And there's nothing wrong with wanting any of those things, of course—we did them all—but I sometimes feel like I'm half asleep.

The other night, I looked over at him, and his face looked masklike, as unreal as my life here often seems. He's a lot younger than you, of course, and his skin is still a young man's skin. When we're kissing and I open my eyes and see him, it takes me a second to orient myself. My mind tries to make him into you, and there's an adjustment period, like when you walk out into sunlight and your pupils contract and briefly, you see white.

I didn't mind it, your age. You had the kind of face that needed to be a little weathered, a little warped, before it took on its true shape. At twenty-six, even thirty, you would have looked unfinished.

That spike lavender smell, I later learned, never came out. The vapors worked into your palms' creases, sunk beneath your fingernails, crept into your hair follicles, tinged the skin behind your earlobes. I grew to like it. I miss it still.

Last night, a neuroscientist who researches human relationships gave a lecture in Centennial Hall. He talked about the neurochemical basis of human bonding. He asked us to close our eyes and remember a time when we felt close to someone, and I thought of the night you met me at the Plough and Stars. Snow was accumulating on the roads when you drove there, fat flakes drifting lazily down and sticking. You called to say you might be late, and I said maybe you shouldn't come, but you said no, you'd be fine. A local bluegrass band was playing—the singer wore a porkpie hat, and the accordionist a bushy beard—and we drank beer until the bar closed. When we stumbled out at 2 a.m., the white was blinding. Drifts of snow three feet tall, airy and loose, not that biting grainy stuff, but fairyland snow. Spun like cotton candy.

The city was muffled. An almost imperceptible hiss, that soft fizzing noise the ice crystals make as they compact and melt, was all we could hear between the crunch of our footsteps. At the row of meters where you'd parked, we couldn't make out which car was yours. You had to brush snow from license plates. Digging it out would've taken a shovel and an hour. We left the car shrouded in its heavy wet blanket and walked the fifteen blocks to your apartment. The traffic lights were blinking yellow, the way they do when whoever controls such things decides it's best to give up. The streets were empty, even Mass Ave and Broadway. We left the sidewalks and walked in the roads. I leaned on you as we walked, struggling to stay upright, marveling. Snow everywhere: piled on roofs, outlining telephone wires, drifting against street signs. Overhead, the branches of the trees weighted with snow, sagging and sculptural. Snow made its way down my jacket's neck and into my boots, but I didn't care. The world was new, transfigured, lovely, and we were in it together.

The next morning, we woke to cold air leaking through your window sashes—the old wood having shrunk from the glass, the panes loose and rattly—and the hiss of the radiator. Frost had scrawled snowflakes on the windowpanes. The recorded message on the lab's weather hotline said work was delayed, so we crawled back into bed and slept another hour. When we woke, you reached for me beneath the blankets, and we had sex, layers of wool and down piled on us, and I thought of the snow's weight and imagined we were moving beneath it. It was then that you said you liked to imagine me pregnant, and that became a thing I imagined for us, too.

This month is better than last month, which was better than the month before. When I went home for Christmas, I flew into Boston and rented a car, and I thought about driving by your apartment, maybe texting you, seeing whether you were around and wanted to go for a walk, just to catch up, just as friends, but of course I didn't. I knew better than to reverse whatever progress I've made, and I do think there has been some.

Sometimes I'm not sure I want to let go. There's something sad about leaving sadness behind. If I miss you every day, it means at least there's something I want. You get dimmer and dimmer in my memories, though. I dream about you and wake, feeling a clutching in my chest as you fade, a person flattening into a paper doll.

• • •

The Center for Creative Photography is featuring photographs from the private holdings of an art collector named Stéphane Janssen right now, and Javier took me to see the show yesterday afternoon. This one photograph made me think of you. Two boys stand by a rainy window, one leaning in to lick the glass, tongue a pink spoon, the other pressing his palm to the pane. The photographer is inside, the boys outside. The boy whose mouth is open, his gaze is both intimate and guarded, as if he's challenging whoever holds the camera.

I never told you this, but I didn't like your paintings. I didn't understand them. I know it's a reductive way to look at art, but I couldn't figure out how your work had come from you. You were charismatic. People liked to watch you, they liked being around you. There's a girl here in my program who's very pretty, with high cheekbones and a pinched, aristocratic-looking nose; the other night she was telling a story at a bar, and she reminded me so much of you I felt caught off guard. At first it seemed odd—you look nothing alike; your face's sturdiness couldn't be further from her delicate, thin bone structure—but then I realized why: when she tells stories, she looks into the distance. It's the gaze of an actress performing for her audience, lit with the certainty they are looking at her. That's the way you told stories, with rapture in your face.

But your paintings—it was as if you wanted to renounce that quality. They were small, squalid things, boxy and dark. Oil slicks shaped with a ruler. Looking at them took effort. Not because they repelled the eye—though they did—but because the viewer could sense the source of the unease lurking beneath the surface and to make yourself keep looking, sensing that something might rise up, was difficult. Maybe that's what made your work good. It's probably also what made it hard to sell. Who wants unease hanging over their living room couch?

I say I didn't like those paintings, but I couldn't look away from them, either. They made me feel like we were in a staring contest, and I didn't want to back down. I never did see what was beneath those tarry surfaces. Did you know? One time, I sat alone in your apartment for an hour, just looking at a painting of yours and wondering that. Finally, I decided you didn't know, and that was why you kept painting them. Have you figured it out yet? If you did, would it change anything?

I didn't know it when I moved here, but Tucson is a low-light zone. Storefront lights are regulated. Streetlights too. You can see the stars even when you are in the middle of the city, if such a sprawling city can be said to have a middle. The buildings are stunted, mostly one- or two-story—even the commercial buildings in the business district—and spread across the sand like moss. At first, I thought it was creepy, all the dark streets, as if the city had died. When you're driving in a neighborhood you don't know, you sometimes have to roll down your window and shine a flashlight on the street signs. But now I think it's kind of lovely. You park and get out and look up from all that darkness at the smattering of stars above. It's like being in the Berkshires.

I went for a walk tonight by myself to clear my head. My advisor said this afternoon that he thinks the work I'm doing is promising, that he sees me going on to have a good academic career if that's what I want. A year ago, I would've been thrilled, and I was happy, but more and more I'm not sure what's important. On my walk, I saw three coyotes trotting up Bean Avenue, tails angled low, and I envied them even though I knew they'd been forced out of their habitat by developers, driven into the city by bulldozers and concrete.

My advisor said more: he wants me to go with him to Boston next year. Harvard has offered him a prestigious one-year fellowship, and he can bring a research assistant. I could live in university housing not far from your apartment, take the year to focus on research. It's a great opportunity, too good to turn down, really. When I told him I needed to think about it, he laughed and said, "Think about what exactly, Kate?"

I didn't realize how much we drank until we split up. So many nights spent in that bright, off-kilter glow. You'd cook paella, and I'd help you make aioli, dripping the olive oil as you whisked the egg yolks, and we'd invite people over—your friends, really, who all seemed to be European, though you'd grown up in New Hampshire—and talk and laugh and eat until we were past buzzed, headachy and yawning, and the evening was about to break. Or we'd go to a dinner party in the South End or a repurposed warehouse on A Street by the wharf. There was always this urgency, this sense we had to get in as much as we could. I guess maybe it was a problem.

I don't miss the way we fought those nights. I forget that, sometimes. The way you'd grab my forearms when I went to leave, distraught, hold me so I couldn't go, your thumbs sinking into the soft part of my arm below the tendon. The way I'd pull away to feel your hands tighten. That was, of course, what I wanted: for you to make me stay. Afterward, you'd run a thumb down the trough of skin and fatty tissue, turn my hands up, kiss my palms. And then, often—usually—we'd have sex. In my memory every time is the time you took me by the shoulders and turned me, leaned me on the mattress in your entryway hall that was propped at a 45-degree angle, one of your arms crooked around my ribcage, the other bracing us against the coils. When I closed my eyes, I almost felt I was lying down. Then I'd feel the mattress's wobble, your breath on my neck, and remember that we were tilted, and dizziness would overtake me, and I'd focus on breathing and the point where our bodies met, which seemed like the only stable thing.

Of course, it was us that was moving. It only looked like the world.

If only we'd met each other later, you liked to say, maybe things would've been different. The distance, the fighting, it was because you felt guilty about falling in love with me when you were living with another woman. I don't know if I believe that. If you'd loved me enough, I sometimes think, you would've gotten over the guilt. Other days, I think nothing's that simple, especially not the human heart.

You know how there are moments you keep going back to in your mind when you are trying to answer an unanswerable question? For me, it's that morning your ex-girlfriend called you six times in a row, then buzzed your bell. You'd been so distant that week, and when she showed up, I thought I knew why. The fear on your face—I'd never seen it before. It was like you were facing the death of something, and I guess you were. I thought you wanted me to go. You certainly didn't say anything to stop me. I didn't go home, couldn't face sitting inside, trapped, while you said to her whatever you had to say. I went for a long walk instead and then to the movies by myself, and that's why I didn't hear you when you came to my apartment, knocked and called to me, sat outside on that cracked, peeling linoleum for an hour, waiting.

You'd pushed notes under my door. That's how I knew you'd been by: the row of torn white notes. One of them says, "I love you more than I've ever loved anyone. Please open the door." You thought I was angry. I wasn't, of course, just sad. But what were you? I'm still not sure. Sometimes, I take that note out, look at it, and see just what you say: that you loved me. Other times, I don't see love at all. It's like one of those optical illusions, where you see a woman's face and then a vase and then a woman's face again. Or a box, and at first it's open at the top and then at the side. Even though I know how they work, those pictures always make me dizzy.

I've put the note away. But the words, those I can't put away. Some nights, I lie in bed and think about you in my old hallway and that note—and blink, it means one thing; blink, it means another.

Even leaving doesn't solve the problem of leaving. I read that somewhere. It seems about right.

I told my advisor no today. No, I won't be going to Boston. "Is this because of Javier?" he asked. "Because if it is, you're making a mistake." It wasn't Javier, I told him, and I felt sure I wasn't making a mistake.

I'll be staying in Arizona next year. It's official; the position has been offered to another research assistant, and he's accepted. It was foolish on my part, and necessary. After this, I can't imagine anything will bring me back to Boston.

Andy called yesterday, said things were good at the lab and my old coworkers missed me, and then he mentioned that he'd run into you, that you'd asked after me. "Oh," I said. "He's still in love with you," he said, and the twisting in my stomach felt like the onset of a migraine. I can't tell you how badly I wanted to believe him, and more than that, to believe it might make a difference. It doesn't, I know. I see you sitting outside my old apartment door, pushing those notes underneath, and I know it doesn't.

There are so many things I know now, things I wish I could tell you.

You might know that the name of the saguaro cactus, the long skinny cactus that looks like it's reaching out its arms, is said with a silent *g*. You might even know that they are run through with wooden ribs. Architects use the ribs sometimes. You wouldn't know that they bloom, though. I didn't know myself until last month, when I saw rows of saguaro in Sabino Canyon, each wearing a saucer-sized creamy white blossom like a tiara. The centers are yellow. Some cacti have a single blossom, some clusters. The flowers open at night and close by midday, driven shut by the heat. Or is it the light? I guess it could be the light.

The last time I saw you was nothing special. Eight a.m. on a Tuesday morning. Late winter, and the sky was cloudy, the sidewalks slushy, icy and thawing. My wet hair was tied up with a rubber band. I was headed down the concrete steps to the Central Square T, the side entrance by Pearl Street. You'd waited for me on that little landing halfway down—knowing I'd be on my way to Kendall Square, to work—and I almost started to take the second flight of stairs without seeing you. Then you said my name. I just stood there, stupidly. Commuters jostled by. You looked at me and smiled that sad, sheepish smile. Then you held out your arms and said, "I had to see you."

I couldn't move. Water from my hair dripped onto my neck and trickled down my shirt. I remember thinking that not drying my hair was a bad habit. You took a step toward me, and I said, "Don't touch me," and took a step backward. I jostled a woman wheeling a battered plaid suitcase, and she glared. While I was apologizing to her retreating shoulders as she bumped the suitcase down the stairs to the turnstiles, you took my arm. I went stiff. I felt like my heart was in that ugly suitcase, being rolled away.

You said, "Please, baby," and I said, "I can't," and we looked at each other, each searching the other's face for what we wanted—which I think was the same thing, a reason to change our minds—and then I pulled my arm from your grasp. I walked down the stairs, and I didn't look back. Sometimes I think if I had, I would have run back to you, and this story would be different. I can't seem to shake that thought, even though I know it's unlikely. Even though I know that really what would've happened is that I would have run back, and the story would be the same.

· II ·

Never Gotten, Never Had

ESME IS COMING, and it can only be a mistake. She has left her graduate program, dissertation begun and abandoned, and now she is drifting around the country while her fiancé completes an assignment in Rome. She met him at Stanford. The two things she tells me about him on the phone when she announces the news of their engagement and her plan to visit me are that he is taller than her, even if she is wearing heels, which is not a hard thing to be and suggests he is in fact short, and that he wants to go to business school, preferably to Wharton, after he finishes his PhD in computer science, which he is on track to do next year. They'll see at that point what their options are, she says, and I am tempted to say, but don't, "So the first-person plural begins this early, huh." Her voice is triumphant, excited, and when I ask about her decision to give up on getting a doctorate herself, she says airily, "Oh, there are no jobs."

"But wouldn't you like the satisfaction of knowing you did it?"

"Did something stupid? No."

"If you love it, it isn't stupid."

"I don't."

"You did."

"It's all archives and libraries. I wanted to read and travel, and I can do that without getting a useless degree. If I have to write one more grant application, I'll throw myself off a bridge, I swear to god. Not that you shouldn't finish yours. Science is different. It's practical."

How long is she thinking of staying, I ask. What I don't say is that this is not a great time. Javier has moved in, because he asked to, eight months into dating, and I stalled, and when he finally said it was obvious I wasn't into it, meaning moving in but maybe also our whole relationship, I felt panicked and bad and said yes, of course I wanted to live together, I was just nervous about my landlord's reaction, and now here we are, two people sharing an apartment too small for the both of us—or rather, too small for him and me and my doubts.

Not long, she says, maybe two weeks.

"Two weeks?" I say, in what I hope is a neutral tone.

"We can go hiking," she says, and I can see this whole thing is doomed.

Esme's flight gets in at 2 p.m., and she does not offer to arrange to take a cab, so I take the afternoon off at the lab and wait in the little cell phone lot by the airport until she calls to say she's landed, sounding peeved that they're still taxiing. "I mean, how big can this airport be?" she asks, and when I ask if she should get off her phone since the plane is in motion, she says impatiently, "I'm sure it's fine." "I'm a mess," she continues. "My skin is so dry, I'm afraid to look in the mirror. I cannot *wait* to be off this plane."

But when Esme comes out of the sliding glass doors into the desert heat, she looks cool and composed and pleased to see me. She waves, props her sunglasses on her head, pulling back her blonde hair, recently highlighted and longer than normal. Because it is silky and fine, like a child's, she usually wears it in a shaggy bob, but now it touches the tops of her shoulder blades, visible in her filmy white tank top, which billows loosely above her dark-wash jeans. Her skin looks dewy, not dry, and her cheeks are flushed. Dropping out of graduate school agrees with her.

"Let's get tacos," she says, after she throws her bags in the trunk.

"Tacos it is."

"And horchata."

But at the restaurant, she orders only a nopales salad.

"Still water with ice?" the waiter asks when she asks for water, and she says, "Sparkling, if you have it. If you don't, no problem: I'm easy."

"So have you begun planning the wedding?" I ask.

The restaurant is quiet, the afternoon lunch rush over, and overhead a fan spins in slow circles.

Esme sips her Gerolsteiner.

"The thing about weddings," she begins philosophically, "is that they are an expression of the community as much as they are an expression of the couple, the couple's individual tastes and joint taste. It's beautiful, really. All these people coming together, you, your fiancé, everyone's parents. Stephen's are very involved, and my mother, it turns out, has a lot of ideas too, different ideas from Steven's mother's ideas, which are very particular, even though my parents are paying, so there's all that to contend with, but it could be worse. We agree about the important things: the wedding will be in the south of France, in June, and I get the dress I want, regardless of what it costs, no one's allowed to say anything, and if I don't kill anyone, we'll count it as a success."

"Will your dress be expensive?"

"It's being designed specifically for me."

"So wedding planning is going well."

"*So* well," she says.

The waiter brings her salad, the cactus roasted and tossed with tomatoes and onions and jalapenos, which she picks around, and my enchiladas, which are the best thing on the menu, made with carne seca, a dried beef that is not dry at all, but flavorful, salty, and a little smoky-tasting.

"What do you want to do while you're in town?" I say.

"Oh, anything."

I tell her that we can get a drink at Hotel Congress, a great old hotel downtown, a little rundown, but cool. And we can go to El Presidio, which is a Spanish-influenced neighborhood, and drive up to the foothills too, to see the night sky and the city, striking from above.

"Perfect," she says. "I want to see it all. Mostly, I want to see what your life here is like. Also, I was thinking maybe we could go to Mexico."

"Mexico?" I say.

"Why is that surprising?"

"You realize it's a whole different country."

"You don't need a passport," she says. "Besides, I'm here for two weeks. No offense, you're great company, obviously, but we have to find *some* way to entertain ourselves. And why pass up the chance when it's so close? My friend has a friend who stayed at a resort someplace nearby and loved it. It's supposed to be very affordable."

It turns out Esme has already booked us a room. She tells me this as though I will be excited, though it means I will have to take another three days off, which is not great, and of course I offer to pay for half, an offer she declines, saying magnanimously, "You can get the meals or something. We'll figure it out."

I text Javi while she is in the bathroom. He doesn't respond immediately because he's in the lab, working, where I should be. I think of him in the stuffy, windowless room, joking with the other guys, and it is almost all guys, harassing Tomas, who is always complaining that Hugh has taken his spectrum analyzer, an expensive piece of equipment. Hugh, who is British, likes to act like it's no big deal, but it is. Tomas is the one people harass, though, because he's such a pain about it. Some people are perpetually aggrieved, and Tomas is one of those people, which makes his legitimate grievances harder to treat with sympathy.

"Esme wants to go to Mexico," I write.

"Sounds like a lot," he texts when he responds. We have dropped Esme's bags at our casita, and she has retired to the guestroom for a brief nap. I can hear her on the phone with her fiancé, telling him about the trip and how good the food here is, though she barely ate anything.

"Tell her I can't go."

"She's your friend."

"Why do I have to do everything myself," I type, and he responds with an emoticon face with two *x*'s for eyes, our expression of sympathy.

I know it's a bad idea, but the more I think about going to Mexico with Esme, the more fun it seems: sunshine instead of the dark lab space, time to read instead of work, time with a female friend, who, even if she is a little much, is a woman. We had fun in college sometimes; once we drove to a North Shore beach, spent a night in a hotel with a *Twin Peaks* vibe that we both pretended to believe was haunted. We got sunburned and rubbed aloe lotion all over and took turns applying an ice pack to our chests. For dinner we splurged on lobster, and she showed me how to dismantle the creature and dip the white slivers of flesh in butter, not making me feel stupid for not knowing. Sand turned up in our dorm room for weeks afterward, even though we washed our beach towels and bathing suits the day we returned, but we didn't care. When Javi comes home, I make guacamole and throw together dinner, and we eat in the backyard, candles flickering on the table, the air cooling off now that the sun has gone down.

The resort offers massages and green tea facials. Esme tells me this at dinner, telling Javier that he's invited, too.

"It's a critical time right now," he tells her. He is relaxed, enjoying having company, the two of us, and she has been charming him with stories about the fruit trees in her yard in Palo Alto, laden with figs and oranges.

"I think it should be fine," I say.

He looks at me, surprised.

"You never take time off," he says. "You said that you wanted to go hard this year, that this year was your big push."

Since he moved in, I've been working long hours, going in on the weekends, rivaling the notoriously hard-working Chinese students for the most hours in the lab. The Australians are the most laid back; everyone does their part to live up to their culture's stereotypes, except for Xian, who has long hair and hangs out with the Australians and likes to smoke weed and read surfing magazines. We all think he's going to drop out, and secretly I admire him more than I admire Javi, who works hard, but responsibly hard, always in by 8 a.m., always out by 6.

"Well, I know," I say. "But Esme's only here this once."

"Let her take a break, Javier," Esme says. "She's obviously been working too hard. She always did in college, and no one likes a grind."

"You're one to talk," I say. "You graduated summa cum laude and went to Stanford, like, immediately."

"I'm just saying you should relax," Esme says. "I promise you, people will like you more. It makes you more creative too, all the studies say so. Don't think of it as a break from your research, think of it as a contribution to it."

"But you're getting close," Javier says to me. My most recent experiments have been going well, and he's right: I should just press on. I'm working on cooling down mercury with a laser and doing a spectroscopic analysis, examining the scattered light to help develop a better neutral atom clock, and I'm finally getting somewhere. It's more a question of momentum than anything though, and a few days off won't change that, I tell myself, even though a superstitious feeling in me says it might. The energy that should be propelling me forward isn't there; doing iteration after iteration is beginning to drive me a little crazy, the tests invading my sleep so that when I wake up, I feel convinced I've already put in a full day of work, and, exhausted, my actual day takes on the quality of a dream.

"The data will be there when I get back," I say. "I doubt the physical world will change too much in the few days we're gone."

When Esme excuses herself to talk to her fiancé, Javier says to me, "This isn't like you." "I can be a lot of ways," I tell him. "I guess this is one of them." I need a break, I say, and who knows, maybe a little time away *will* actually make me more creative, and doesn't he think it's important to rest, to find some sort of balance? He is normally mild and encouraging, but he shakes his head. "When did you say she was leaving again?" he says. When I begin to respond, he says, "Don't answer that. It was rhetorical."

I work hard the next few days, leaving Esme to entertain herself. She takes the car, does some exploring, much of it, I can see from the shopping bags mounting in the guestroom, commercial in nature. At night, she talks with her fiancé. She has planned the trip to Mexico for the weekend, a concession to my schedule. "We can go down Friday, come back Tuesday. That way, we'll basically have three days. The drive is like seven hours," she says. "We don't want to get there and have to turn right around and come back."

Javi takes over cooking, complains that he is the one entertaining Esme.

I did the same for his brother, I reply.

Yes, he retorts, but he's nicer.

We stand around the table in the lab, both wearing protective glasses. With all the steel and polished surfaces, a misaimed laser could damage the eyes. The table on which we mount equipment floats, held aloft by air pistons. I push it down, and it makes a pssst noise as it self-corrects.

He is in a bad mood because his experiment isn't going well. He can't tell whether it's him or the equipment, and the lab boss won't buy him the equipment he needs.

Maybe he shouldn't have moved in, he says, maybe I wasn't ready.

"It's like you're avoiding me," he says. "You're never home, and now you're going to Mexico without me. Does it matter if we live together if we never see each other?"

"We're together all the time at the lab," I say. "And you were invited to Mexico, you just didn't want to go. You could still come." Saying this, I half hope he will, because I am nervous about being alone with Esme, managing her needs, and half hope he won't.

"It's a girls' thing," he says. "I'm not really invited. Esme doesn't want to drink mimosas and get a face mask with me."

"A facial," I say.

"Whatever," he says. But he adjusts the strap on my glasses when he walks by, tightening them so they don't slip, and when he goes out for lunch, he brings back my favorite tacos from the taco place he doesn't like as much as I do.

On Friday morning, Esme and I leave for Mexico, the temperature climbing quickly toward a hundred. I drive, Esme navigates, and she is good at it, tracking our progress on the map with a focus I remember from college. At the border, we present our licenses and the woman waves us through, and immediately, the road grows more shoddily paved, the signs smaller and less frequent. Twenty-one kilometers down the road, we stop at the Instituto Nacional de Migración office and do our entry paperwork, which Esme has researched thoroughly. We don't go into an office but walk up to a window at a kiosk. Esme presents a folder of documents that the bored official behind the desk, a man in a linen shirt who chats with his coworkers, does not want to see.

We continue on, and the highway narrows, a straight thin line through the tan countryside, toward and past Hermosillo, which everyone says is an ugly city. For a while we listen to music, and then we turn it off and talk. Esme says that her mother-in-law has been calling her about the wedding all week, wanting to know if she's chosen flowers yet, even though she has told her a million times that that's for next month.

"Did you know that in Europe in the Middle Ages, women had to escape the sin of Eve by becoming celibate or becoming mothers? Nun or bride, those were the two options," she says.

"I thought Eve's sin had to do with knowledge."

"Disobedience."

"Right, and then came the knowledge."

"It was a grim time. You weren't supposed to be too into having sex with your wife, or else you were treating her like a prostitute. Even being too in love with your wife made you an adulterer." "Unsurprisingly," she adds, "there was a popular saying: No man marries without regretting it."

"No woman either, I bet."

"On that, the record is silent."

We stop for lunch, the heat intense. We drink bottled water, sparkling, because why not, and play fuck, marry, kill. "Posh Spice, Sporty Spice, Baby Spice," she says.

"Kill Baby."

"And?"

"Kill them all."

"Not an option."

"Fuck Posh, then, because she'd be too high maintenance to marry."

When it's Esme's turn, she begins with who she would marry, puzzling over the benefits, and working her way to kill.

"Marry the navy because then you could get a boat; fuck the marines, for obvious reasons; and kill the air force."

"The air force has the best quality of life, supposedly."

"Sure, if you want a shitty quality of life."

"It's the best of your options. Think hard, marriage is forever."

"Depends on how you do it," she says. But as far as I can tell, she has no qualms about Stephen, and every time he calls, she gets this dreamy look on her face, a softness of expression that I haven't seen on her before.

• • •

The resort is maybe the nicest place I've ever stayed, our room's plaster walls painted yellow, large carved teakwood doors opening to a balcony and garden, green and lush. We kick off our shoes and the cool terra-cotta floor feels like a breeze. On the twin beds, the white covers look luxuriously simple, and above are dark wood rafters and two arched windows with dark wood frames and shutters. A fireplace for the colder months sits empty of firewood, potted ferns arching on either side.

Outside, flowers are in bloom, pinks and oranges nodding in the twilight.

"Worth the drive," Esme says.

"What do you want to do now?" I ask.

"Call Stephen and tell him about this place."

I call Javier too, using her phone's international plan, because I feel that I should, and am a little relieved when he doesn't answer.

We spend the next day by the pool, drinking cocktails. The water is cool, but not cold, and we swim and talk about college, take turns rubbing sunscreen on each other's backs, going to the bar to get more drinks. By the time late afternoon comes, we're tipsy, and we take naps and decide to eat at the hotel instead of venturing into town. "Would it be awful to stream a movie?" Esme says. We have finished dinner, are discussing what to do. "We should at least make it a Mexican movie," I say, but she wants to watch an American movie about weddings, starring a wide-eyed Katherine Heigl.

"I used to have this book called *How to Be a Teenage Model*," I tell Esme, "which my second cousin gave to me, after she gave up on her own modeling potential, I guess, and one of the rules was that your eyes should be wide set. One and a half of an eye's worth of space between your actual eyes."

Esme examines her own face in the mirror by the bed. "Another thing to worry about before the wedding," she says. "Some bridesmaid you are."

In the morning, I wake up early, a little hung over, having slept poorly, and wander out into the acres of land around the hotel with a cup of coffee, watching the rising sun hit the misty lavender slopes of the Sierra Madre in the distance. I remember measuring my own face, consulting the various rules about what created beauty and feeling shame both about where I fell short and where I did not, the helplessness of watching my body become what it would become with so many consequences, it sometimes seemed, and so little control. But Esme seems to have control, she seems to know what to do with what power she has and it seems to have brought her happiness, and while I don't envy her many things, I do envy her that.

We eat breakfast and get massages with a sea salt scrub, which Esme insists is her treat and which are a little too vigorous for me, make me feel like I am being buffed away to nothing, though Esme seems to like it—"I feel like a *newborn*," she says with satisfaction afterward, "like one of those featherless baby birds, all pink and naked"—and, in the late afternoon, take a tour of the nearby village, with its Andalusian architecture. Cypress trees shimmer against the white walls of churches and other buildings, narrow green arrows pointing toward the blue sky.

Our guide is a patient and knowledgeable middle-aged woman with a thick blonde braid and a stylish straw hat, willing not to make us feel like tourists so much as interested friends. Serrated by the mountain range, the horizon is visible, and a wind that seems to originate there moves over us. Deep red flowers festoon a spindly bush that grows near many of the buildings, its tendrils drifting across doorways, and the air smells fragrant.

We walk and walk and eventually Esme gets a blister and says she wants to leave the tour early, and I know enough not to argue. We sit at a café and drink lemonade.

At dinner, we order a feast, many little vegetable starters, a soup made with manta ray and shrimp, beef enchiladas, chicken gorditas, camarones a la parrilla, churros and flan, glasses of wine and bacanora, like tequila, we are told, but only available in Sonora, and, at the end of the night, a pitcher of margaritas that never comes.

The bill arrives.

"I'll get this," I say.

Esme takes the bill from my hand, scrutinizes it. She waves to the waitress, points to the charge for the pitcher.

"We're still waiting on this," she says, "but we don't want it anymore."

"So you never got the margaritas."

"Never gotten, never had," Esme says.

The waitress brings me back the bill, the margaritas removed. Esme checks to be sure it's been done correctly before allowing me to pay. We leave the restaurant, and I am pleasantly exhausted, looking forward to bed, but then Esme sees a dive bar and decides she wants to go in.

"This is sort of like my bachelorette," she says.

"This is nothing like your bachelorette," I say, but I follow her anyway.

Neither of us speaks much Spanish, and in this bar, the bartender does not know much English, so we end up with beers neither of us especially wants. They taste watery, and at least there isn't much alcohol in them, I think. Rather than shout over the din, we sing along to the jukebox, though we don't know the words. We wave off the men who keep trying to talk to us, claiming we are both married. We can't stop laughing, and I am not sure whether either of us is having a good time or whether we just believe we should be, and whether that's enough. When we get back to the hotel, Esme and I have both had too much to drink after too much sun, and we collapse on our beds fully clothed, fall sleep like that without saying goodnight, smearing the pillowcases with our eyeliner.

Our third day, we recover, lie by the pool again. Instead of cocktails, we drink water with our Advil. She calls Stephen, I call Javier, and we read books, out of things to say to each other, maybe. "I wish we had a TV," she says, and when I suggest we could play a game, having found a set of old board games in our wardrobe, she shrugs, goes back to looking at a wedding magazine.

. . .

On the drive back, we review the fun we had, starting to shape the stories we will tell, listen to the radio. At the border, the line of cars is long, and she begins to ask me about Javier, whether I think we'll get married. I tell her I don't know, and she asks me a series of questions about his background and his job prospects and his life goals and where I might fit in, each question more pointed, and when it's our turn, the border guard is not interested in us, waves us through, and Esme says, "I mean, it makes sense, right, you two are *living* together," and I am so nervous I turn into the holding area for additional searches by accident. A uniformed man asks for my ticket, the ticket that explains why we have been sent here, and when I try to explain it was all a mistake, I was not given a ticket, he grows suspicious and grim and makes us get out of the car. While we wait for him to finish going through the trunk and the border dog to smell us and the car and our luggage, now on the pavement, Esme says, "My advice is to tell him which ring you want in advance. Or tell him to ask me, and you can tell me and I'll tell him, that's probably the best way." Stephen has given her his grandmother's pearl ring, and it's clear she likes the story but also wishes that he had gotten her the ring she designed in her mind, with tiny smoky diamonds set around a central brilliant-cut one. Maybe for an anniversary, she tells me, maybe their first one. "I *deserve* a big diamond," she says.

When I say something about disliking how American women are encouraged to calculate their own worth, she stops speaking to me.

By the time we arrive in Tucson, we are on better terms because I have apologized and mollified her by asking a bunch of questions about her honeymoon and because it would be too awful for her to have to book an earlier flight and leave. Contrite, we both spend the next few days being warm to each other, and careful, and when she mentions hiking again, I say "Sure!" in a cheery way, without a trace of skepticism. Javi says he wants to come too, that he needs sunlight, so on Saturday we all drive to Gate's Pass, even though it is insanely hot. We time our hike for the evening, when it cools off a little and the sun sets, turning the sky a brilliant yellow and orange, silhouetting the mountains and desert flora, saguaros and fishhook barrels and the round puffy pincushion cacti.

A storm arrives around 3 p.m. Lightning opens the sky, the flash of light a doorway into another world, and maybe a better one. By 6 p.m., though, the sky is clear, the roads passable. On the drive, the air is freshened with velvet mesquite and creosote, and the hike itself we pass in quiet contemplation, passing a canteen of water back and forth. As we stand at the top of the ridge in silence watching the sunset, I remember a party in college when, having had too much to drink, I'd gotten the spins, and Esme's boyfriend had helped me into the bathroom, where I'd sat on the floor, leaning against him, unable to throw up, and we'd both listened to her flirting with another guy outside the door. He'd rested his cheek on my head and said to me sadly, "She doesn't love me, does she." "She does, in her way," I'd said, trying to reassure him, but we both knew I was lying. Esme is probably remembering transgressions I myself have made, in her eyes, and Javi, well, who knows what he is thinking. I can never really tell.

The night before she leaves, Esme says she wants to meet my friends, so when Hugh texts to say people are gathering at his apartment complex, which has a pool, I convince Javier to go with us. Everyone is hanging out, drinking. We swim, dry off, go up to Hugh's apartment to continue the fun. Late into the evening, Esme slides onto my lap, straddling me. I am sitting on a couch, talking to Xian, and this surprises me. I am not sure what to do; she is so light, but I don't want to push her off. She seems easy to hurt, and I don't want to risk that. "What are you doing?" I say. Instead of answering, she lifts my hair from my neck and leans in and kisses me. My mouth responds, as if on autopilot; it is only polite. The pressure of her lips is shockingly faint. It's like being kissed by a ghost, kissing back like trying to locate a ripple of water by touch. Is this how men feel when they kiss me? I wonder. Her tongue darts in my mouth, a small minnow, and I can feel this is a performance for the men. Or maybe for herself, her last wild experience before marriage.

A low whistle from across the room.

I push her away, my hands on her small shoulders.

"You're engaged," I say, and she laughs.

Javi drives us home, sober and tolerant. He saw the whole thing but seems to understand what happened as not a threat, maybe because he can tell how drunk Esme is and what a show-off she is too, or maybe because he is good at hiding things. We both are, until we're not. I'm sorry for a lot of things. I want to want him, but I don't. I want my ex-boyfriend or Xian, or a number of other people, but not him, this gentle man who loves me. We say good night to Esme and get ready for bed, him in his T-shirt, me in his T-shirt too.

He reaches for me, and I pull away.

"That thing with Esme, is that what you want?"

"No," I say.

"What *do* you want?" he asks.

And I lie awake a long time in the dark, thinking about that, wishing my body could do the necessary thing, though it can't, thinking about what it means to be afraid you might be killed by a person you love and what it means to be afraid that your own desire for a person will be the thing to explode and kill you.

"I wish I knew," I say at last, but he has already fallen asleep.

The Sea Latch

WHEN I WAKE our first day at the Sea Latch, my mother and teenage sister sit on the motel's carpeted porch, smoking as they gaze over the railing at the passing cars. The sound of the Atlantic Ocean's slow suck carries across the motel parking lot. Route 1, the coastal highway that runs through York, passes directly in front of the motel. You can see the highway's glittering gray pavement and the boardwalk's sandwich stands, but not the water. Still, the salt-air smell makes its way to us, the wind that carries it over the dunes bracing and wet and alive.

"Should we head to the beach?" I ask. Late yesterday afternoon, we arrived amid a July squall that lasted until dark, but the morning sky is clear, the air balmy.

"I think I'm just going to sit by the pool," my mother says. The swimming pool, ringed by a chain-link fence, occupies the middle of the motel parking lot.

"But the beach is so close," I say. "We could see the ocean."

"I can hear it from the pool." She and Agnes glance at each other.

"Okay," I say. "The pool it is."

"You go ahead," my mother says. "We'll catch up." My sister looks straight ahead, blowing smoke over the wrought-iron railing of the raised concrete porch. A car rolls by, squeezing through the narrow space between our row of rooms—which forms an island in the motel complex—and the outer horseshoe of rooms across the way.

Agnes tilts her chair back. She looks luminous in the morning sun, her olive skin taking on that filtered-light quality of amber, though she's broken out, and a faint red trail of pimples traces her forehead. Her belly rolls over her sweatpants, a plump white coast of skin. She is four months along and starting to show. She posted the news on MySpace—"About me: preggers"—and that was how I found out. Trying her TracFone, I found another girl's voice on the voicemail greeting, another girl's name. When I called home, dialing Vermont from Tucson, my mother answered, sounding evasive and distant. I said, "What's new?" and she said, "Oh, not much." I waited, giving her a chance to tell me. She was silent. I said, "Agnes wouldn't happen to be pregnant, would she?" There was a pause, and then, her voice all cheerful belligerence, she said, "Yes, actually, she is."

Farther down on Agnes's MySpace, she'd written: "I get interested in things easily. It's the staying interested that's hard."

"Here," my mother says. She hands me a key. The motel has given us two of the old-fashioned kind, real metal keys attached to oval turquoise key fobs. Embossed in white is our room number: 32A. "Agnes and I can share."

She and Agnes wait for me to leave so they can continue their discussion. This is their new thing: they stop talking when I approach, make a half-hearted attempt to pretend I'm not interrupting, and start talking again as soon as I walk away. Mostly, they seem to talk about

Agnes's boyfriend, Tully, whom she met in community college at the beginning of the fall term and is considering breaking up with, and Agnes's ex-boyfriend, Mike, who's joined the army and will deploy to Iraq in a month. Agnes is still in love with him.

I stretch, inhale the salty air, and my stomach makes a low complaint.

"Want to come to the coffee shop with me?" I ask Agnes. She might want breakfast, I think, though my mother will not. My mother's sole nourishment is a microwaveable Hungry Man dinner she heats up at 10:00 p.m., a habit I made the mistake of suggesting she reconsider. "You might feel better if you ate regular meals throughout the day," I said, and now she calls breakfast, lunch, and dinner, if eaten before ten, my "regular meals."

"No, thanks," Agnes says. She glances at her belly and tugs down her tank top.

"Going to have a—" my mother begins.

"Yep," I say.

"Enjoy," she says.

My mother likes to say she hasn't been in a major city since 1976. That was the year she married my father. In the almost twenty years since they divorced, she hasn't dated, she hasn't eaten at a restaurant other than the Steak Out ("We made a deal with the bank: they won't serve steaks and we won't cash checks"), and she hasn't been on vacation. She didn't even fly to Florida when her father was on his deathbed. She debated and debated as he lapsed into delirium. Then she decided he wouldn't want her to go, knowing as he did how anxious travel made her. I'd been sent as a proxy. He died while my plane was crossing Mississippi.

So now we have come to see the ocean, using a portion of the money from my grandfather's estate to fund this family vacation, our first in more than a decade. Javi and I had planned to spend this July in Madrid, where I expected he would propose, and I'd already arranged for time off at the lab, so when we admitted the obvious—although we did not fight, some part of me remained unavailable to him and was perhaps becoming unavailable to me, too, and things could not continue—I decided to fly home for a week, check in, leave Arizona and our friends' solicitousness and puzzlement. Emboldened by her small inheritance, my stubborn, generous mother wants to celebrate my visit home by seeing the elemental New England landscape she loves and talks about a lot but hasn't visited since Agnes and I were born. Her dream for retirement, she has long said, is "to buy a white house high up on a hill, so I can see the waves crashing against the rocks." "Why white?" I asked her once. "That's how I see it," she said, "in my mind's eye," and she turned her face away and smiled. I want this for her, badly. It is the one wish for the future I've heard her express. But no money is in sight beyond her tiny disability check, which she collects for a depression that often immobilizes her and necessitates a raft of medication, and she's running through the inheritance fast, so this three-day trip seems likely to be the closest she'll get to owning that house.

On the drive to York Beach yesterday, we were quiet. My mother doesn't like the radio, so the only sounds in the car were the wind through the window she cracked for fresh air and the faint hum of Agnes's ancient Discman. Two hours in, the road forked unexpectedly, and a detour sign directed us to go right. My mother turned where the sign indicated, muttering "Goddamnit" to herself. Fifteen miles down this new route, the road signs said we were headed west, not east. We stopped at a Shell station for directions. As she put the car in park, my mother's face looked bloodless. Seeing that she was rattled, I offered to go in myself, but she said, "Wait here." When she came out, her hands were shaking, but she sat in the driver's seat examining the hand-drawn map, restarted the engine, and a few turns later we were heading east again. "Nice work, Mom," Agnes said, and my mother smiled at the two of us briefly, glancing over at Agnes beside her, looking at me in the rearview mirror.

Leaving my mother and Agnes smoking, I walk to the motel's main building. The coffee shop advertised on the motel website turns out to be three plastic tables in the lobby. You can buy a Styrofoam cup of coffee for fifty cents, packaged pastries for a dollar. Refills are free.

A freckled blonde girl who looks about Agnes's age, nineteen, sells me a coffee and a well-preserved cheese Danish. She wears homemade cutoffs; her tawny hair glows where the sun has bleached the dark blonde to a pale mother-of-pearl. Her mouth makes a pretty, unaffected moue as she concentrates, filling the cup to the brim. After she hands me the coffee, saying, "Careful! It might not be as good as Dunkin' Donuts, but it's as hot," I ask her about popular beaches in the area. York Beach today, another beach tomorrow, I'm thinking: make the most of the trip. Old Orchard Beach, the girl says, is only a twenty-minute drive, beautiful, a long stretch of white sand with a historic pier and secluded sections if you want to avoid the summer crowds. She uncaps a ballpoint pen and draws arrows on a glossy tourist map. Agnes will love it, I know; we all will. This is what we've come for, what our mother is using her inheritance to buy. She will see the waves and sand, and the old worry in her face will lift like a veil.

I change into my bathing suit, a teal bikini, in our empty motel room, the stale Danish a stone in my stomach. Adjusting the suit so it covers more of my skin, I realize how long it's been since my family has seen me out of winter clothes, how this bikini will signal that I have moved away and changed. Too late, I wish I'd bought a one-piece in Tucson. The bikini is modestly cut: thick straps, plenty of fabric. Still, I can hear my mother's voice: "There's a girl who thinks she's something."

Crossing the hot, sticky asphalt to the deserted-looking pool, flip-flops adhering to the tar and pulling away with a Velcro-like sound, I spot my mother and sister through the chain-link fence. No one is swimming, and the lifeguard chair sits empty. The GUESTS ONLY sign, hopeful and unnecessary, peels at its laminate edges. My mother lies on a white plastic lounge chair. Agnes perches on the pool's edge, dangling her feet in the water, flipping through a magazine. Her beach towel is draped on the lounger next to my mother, a wet imprint from her butt slowly evaporating. Agnes has always been skinny. Pregnant, she's put weight on her stomach, but her spine shows.

Seeing the two of them behind the fence, I think of the alarm system my mother had installed when I was in high school, with motion sensors and beams of light that crisscross the house like thread. We had nothing valuable to steal. Even if a person broke in, the house was remote, on a dirt road that rescue workers would never reach in time to make a difference. The alarm was a continual reminder that the outside world was chaotic and dangerous. She wanted me and Agnes home, but home wasn't safe. Nowhere was safe. You just had to crouch in your corner of the earth and hope no one noticed you.

The sun beats down, but the air feels cool, maybe seventy-five, an Arizona day in midwinter. At the gate I raise the U-shaped metal bar, ease past the sign, and drag a lounger to where my mother sits. She looks up from her paperback. "Well, look who's here," she says, and resumes her reading. Since moving to Tucson several years ago, I swim almost every day. My mother has this idea I don't like the water, though, and acts mildly surprised any time I venture near.

I lie on my stomach, close my eyes, and try to ignore the chill when a cloud moves across the sun. My mother and sister read. I drift in and out of sleep. The occasional car rumbles past, pumping out exhaust that mixes with the chlorine smell and hangs over us, but the sun feels good, and when the breeze is right you can smell the salty tang of the ocean air. All in all, it isn't unpleasant.

We are alone until a family enters the pool area. The mother, a slight, harried-looking woman in espadrilles and a faded racerback suit, opens a rainbow-colored beach umbrella. Her husband directs the kids—a scrawny boy of eight or nine and a sullen teenaged girl who peers from beneath a fringe of bangs with the resentful squint of a traffic cop—to set up lounge chairs a respectful distance from ours. The woman, unable to plant the umbrella in cement, looks around.

"Now how on God's earth am I supposed to use this thing?" she says in our direction.

My mother tents her book on her stomach. "You'd think an umbrella'd come with a stand," she offers.

"You would," the woman agrees.

Her husband has determined that one of the lounge chairs is broken. He tells the girl to go get another. She slouches around the pool and hauls over a new lounger, stepping slowly, as if pulling a huge weight.

"For what those things cost, they should set themselves up," my mother continues. She is deeply introverted by nature, but she can be voluble with strangers in odd bursts I cannot predict. She'd talked about getting an umbrella for the trip but decided against it when she learned the good ones ran forty to sixty dollars. A large plastic cooler from Walmart was her one concession to luxury: "I'll be damned if I'm going grocery shopping when I'm on vacation," she'd said.

"That's the truth," the woman says, pushing her dark hair from her face.

The boy is climbing the fence. He has the pinched, intelligent face of a smart kid used to being yelled at, and he climbs with an instinctive sureness, barely pausing to find toeholds. Once he's five feet up, clinging to the metal and poised for a fall onto the pool's cracked cement, he lets go with his left hand, unhooks his left foot, and begins to swing like a door.

"Eric, get down from there."

The boy ignores his mother.

"Eric's ADHD," the woman says apologetically. Twisting to look at him, she raises her voice: "I said get down." Eric swings face-first into the fence, tightens his grip.

"So's Agnes," says my mother.

From the edge of the pool, Agnes glances at the woman, then at the boy, now stuck to the fence like a suction toy, and returns to her magazine.

"If it's not the ground, he climbs it."

"Is he on medication?"

"Ritalin and Adderall."

They begin comparing side effects—Ritalin makes Agnes constipated and anxious, Adderall gives Eric swollen glands—as the husband shoves the umbrella in an empty plant container and leans it against the fence. Seeing he's lost the crowd, Eric drops to the pavement, sprints to the pool, jumps in, and begins to paddle in circles, going around and around like a duck with an injured foot. His sister slips earbuds in her ears, which jab through her dark hair, closes her eyes, and sinks into her lounge chair.

The husband joins the conversation. He is a handsome man, slipping into middle age, but not without a certain physical charisma, an ease in his body that suggests an athletic background, perhaps a job as a skilled laborer. My mother smiles at him in a way that tells me she is ready to identify with him, ready to agree. He says, "Tell her about the teacher."

"Oh, the teacher," the wife says. She gives a nervous laugh.

"She said Eric seemed 'troubled' by his relationship with me," the husband says. It is all there, in his voice, the humiliation he must have felt as he took in the statement, hearing it first as himself and then as a wider public looking at a man about whom this was said, and the desire to disprove the implications. But also a bullying quality, an element of blame that attaches to the teacher, to Eric, a refusal to admit responsibility or concern. Poor Eric. Eric paddles stalwartly, though, going in his long circles around the pool, so maybe not; maybe he's impervious to his family's opinion of him. Agnes lays down her magazine and slips into the deep end in one fast, clean move, seconds passing before she reappears at the far side.

The husband lies back on his lounge chair. "Beth and I got married five years ago, and I'm the only father these two know. Like it isn't normal for kids to rebel. 'Troubled.'" He makes a dismissive sound, closes his eyes. "Yeah, well, I'll tell you who'll be troubled, you keep messing with my family. That's what I said to her."

"But not like that," the wife says. "We were very polite, you know, very professional." She leans forward, anxiously looking at her husband, who cannot see her. "We told her that Eric and Rob have a great relationship. That it was the learning disability that made him act out."

"Some people really don't get it," my mother says. The mixture of anger, disdain, and self-righteousness in her voice makes me want to defend the teacher, though for all I know the woman is a total nightmare. I try not to listen to the conversation, which progresses from how stupid the teacher is to how stupid most people are, circling back to the teacher and ending with my mother's pronouncement that what the teacher did was illegal under the Americans with Disabilities Act, the wife's agreement, and the husband's speculation that perhaps a lawsuit is in order. My mother offers her own assessment of Eric's problems and recommends medications to ask the doctor to prescribe. The wife scribbles down these suggestions on the acknowledgments page of my mother's paperback, which she's ripped out and handed to the woman, with a pen.

I rise. "Going in," I say.

"You? Swim?" my mother says. And then, to the wife: "This one never swims." She says it like my not swimming is an honorable but deeply idiosyncratic trait. It is the way she says "regular meals," but without the subtle mockery that suggests I am crazy.

"Wonders never cease," I say.

An aluminum ladder leads into the pool. I descend the steps until my knees are submerged.

Agnes is swimming laps. She swims methodically, each stroke clean and deliberate. In the pool's small shallow end, Eric turns underwater flips. Each time he surfaces, he gasps. Then he flings himself over again. He looks dizzy, and his flips become increasingly crooked.

"Don't puke," the husband yells. "You puke, you don't go in the pool again."

"—a travesty," my mother is saying.

The water is freezing. I plunge in. The last thing I hear before chlorine stings my eyes is my mother saying, "The world is full of small-minded people."

I want not to mind that Agnes is having a baby at nineteen, without being married or finishing college. I want not to mind that she didn't tell me. I do mind, though. I mind a lot. My anger makes me think of a story I heard about a Columbia English professor who put the following question on the final exam: "Part 1: What work this semester did you most dislike? Part 2: What intellectual or emotional flaw in you does this dislike point to?"

On the phone with my mother, I tried to pretend I wasn't pissed that the two of them were sitting in our kitchen in Vermont, chain-smoking and talking about my sister's pregnancy, and that no one had bothered to let me know. I was mad, though. Really mad. And when I'd said, "So when were you planning to tell me?" trying to sound nonchalant, my mother knew. "It wasn't my news to tell," she said.

"Then when was Agnes going to tell me?"

"Maybe I should put your sister on the phone. She's here."

Agnes's voice came through right away, as if she'd been listening at the receiver. "How did you find out?" she asked in a small voice.

"Your MySpace," I said.

"Oh," she said. "I didn't think of that."

"I tried calling. Your phone's disconnected."

"I meant to tell you."

"Well, now I know."

"Yeah," she said. "Now you know."

But I didn't know. Not really. How could I? When I thought of the girl Agnes's ex-boyfriend Mike had gotten pregnant, a girl who lived in a trailer with her mother and the baby and who could easily be my sister, I thought of weedy grass, the scrubby dried-out kind that grows on hard-packed soil. I wanted not to be the person my mother and Agnes thought I was: a person who would judge her for her decision, think she was stupid and backward. But at the same time, I wanted to shake her. How could I not, when I remembered her at five years old, trudging after me up the hill on the way to the school bus in her red rain boots, struggling to keep up? Her hair, a stunning brown, curling around her face and turning gold in the summer, tangling when she climbed from the public pool and the sun began to dry it into waves, so she looked like a sprite? Her beautiful, impish grin, her wild laugh? And our mother, penciling what we owed on the backs of envelopes, figuring and refiguring as though the amounts might change. Our mother, crouched in the corner and waiting it out. I wanted to mail them an invitation, a golden ticket to leave. There's a whole world outside the walls of our house, I wanted to tell my sister. They look like plaster and studs, but really they're paper. Run through, and you'll see.

We've barely spoken since the news. Until last night, that is, after the rain let up and I asked Agnes and my mother if they wanted to get a bite to eat. "No, thanks," my mother said. "I'm a little hungry," Agnes said, glancing at her. "Then go," my mother said.

Agnes and I ambled down the boardwalk as the sun set, looking for a place to stop. Agnes trailed behind me, and I paused to allow her to catch up.

"Sorry," she said, and quickened her pace. We walked side by side for a few minutes, and then she fell behind again.

When we talked on the phone, first she'd said it wasn't planned. Then she said she and her boyfriend Tully hadn't been using birth control for a couple months. "Well, why not?" I'd asked, and she'd said, "I don't know."

At the edge of the beach, a big white hotel with plate glass windows and a wooden deck crowned the rocks. It was an old, sprawling Victorian Greek Revival with bay windows and a wide porch; the hotel's shape suggested a grand interior, many mazelike rooms. The crisp paint job was conservative but lavish in its careful detail, two-toned gray trim with dark, gleaming shutters. It looked as if it had once been a rambling house of the sort my mother described wanting to live in, peopled with a family and a staff and guests, a summer home for the moneyed industrialists who built New England and left their genteel monuments to future generations to salvage and protect as best they could, to rent out to others if they could no longer afford to make a life there of their own. The patio was lit up and lively. I stopped, examined the menu in a display case. The deck, which overlooked the ocean, was full but not packed. Agnes scratched her left ankle with her foot. She looked uncomfortable.

"Here?" she asked.

"Sure," I said. "It's on me."

"Don't you need to be staying at the hotel?"

"Do you need to be staying at the Sea Latch to eat in their coffee shop?"

Agnes tugged on her sweatshirt's frayed cuff, unconvinced.

"Would you rather find a hamburger stand instead?" I asked.

Her face brightened. "Do you want to?" she said.

The hotel's lit windows were inviting. A breeze carried patrons' conversations to us, light and full of promise.

"Sure," I said. "Hamburgers sound good."

We found a stand and ordered, sat at a dirty picnic bench to eat. Agnes dipped a fry in catsup and absentmindedly sucked the catsup from the fry. She stuck it back in the catsup and repeated the process.

"What's Mike up to these days?"

Mike had joined the army to pay child support.

"The same. He says the army's boring. They have to hire a taxi to get off base."

"Does he get to see his kid?"

She sat up straighter. "Yeah, he sees her every weekend when he's home. We're hoping the judge will give him joint custody, though. He wants to go to college when he's done with the army."

"Do you think he'll stay in North Carolina?"

"Nah, he'll move back home."

"Will Tully mind?" Her new boyfriend, the baby's father.

She looked at me, then away. "No," she said. "He knows we're just friends."

After Agnes and I got back from dinner, we watched the small, flickering TV in our room. The yellow was off, making all the people look jaundiced. Agnes and my mother fell asleep shortly after my mother microwaved her dinner. I read in the bathroom until 1:00 a.m., a rolled-up towel wedged under the door to block the light.

• • •

We eat lunch in the motel room, making sandwiches from the mini-fridge. Agnes eats half of hers and two KitKat bars; my mother eats nothing, excusing herself to sit outside and smoke. Agnes joins her as I finish my sandwich: turkey and American cheese on the Pepperidge Farm whole wheat bread my mother bought a loaf of each week of my childhood, which I haven't had since moving to Arizona.

On the motel porch, two old people sit near my mother and Agnes, the man's nose an explosion of red veins. No one talks. "These are the Andersons," my mother says. "From 32B." The redness extends to the man's cheeks, up toward his eyes. He offers me his white plastic patio chair, and though I say no thanks, I'd rather stand, he insists on going to another porch to fetch me one. We all sit in silence long enough for my mother and Agnes to smoke two cigarettes, ashing and drowning the butts in a water bottle my mother's brought. The butts turn the water a muddy color and float like brined animals at a sideshow. The elderly couple rises, says goodbye, and goes to walk the shore.

My mother watches the pair leave the motel grounds, the man reaching for the woman's hand when they come to Route 1 and prepare to cross. The traffic decelerates, stops, and the woman gives a wave to the driver as they make their patient way to the other side.

"You girls done digesting?" my mother asks. "Ready to hit the pool?"

Agnes nods. "Ready as I'll ever be," I say.

The family from earlier is still at the pool, and without the morning breeze to move along the smell of exhaust, it hangs heavy in the air. I quickly grow hot and cranky. I kill time swimming laps, give Eric wide berth. First I swim sidestroke, then breaststroke, then, bored, lie on my back and kick. Agnes stops doing laps long enough to teach me the dolphin kick. She was a swim instructor when she was in community college, and while she isn't generally a patient or focused person, when it comes to water sports, a preternatural calm comes over her.

She shows me how to propel myself along by pushing my pelvis into the water and arching my back, a movement she says looks like a dolphin surfacing for air and that I think looks obscene. Agnes does the kick gracefully, but when I try it, I sink and flail like a drowning mongoose. Agnes watches, diagnoses my problem.

"Pump your butt," she instructs.

"I'm trying," I say.

Eric paddles over, dark hair slicked across his forehead. "Show me," he says.

Agnes demonstrates the kick again for both of us. Eric tries, gets across the pool in a fair approximation of what Agnes did. I try, and sink.

The husband calls to Eric to go. When Eric pretends not to hear him, his mother yells, "You listen to your father or we aren't coming back."

"Will you be at the pool tomorrow?" Eric asks Agnes.

"Sure," she says.

"Good," he says. He climbs the aluminum ladder and trails behind his family as they leave the pool area.

"You cold?" I ask Agnes.

"A little," she says. We get out and towel off, dripping by my mother's lounger.

"What a nice family," my mother says. She stands, too, and stretches. "Well, girls," she says, "I think I've had enough pool time." She collects her book, towel, and sunglasses from the recliner. Agnes packs her beach bag. I pull on jeans over my damp bikini bottom, tug a loose white top over my head. We leave together, and as we exit the gate, while Agnes is turning to slide the U bar into place, I look across the highway to the boardwalk. A breeze twists Agnes's drying hair from her shoulders, and she shivers. "Smell that ocean air," my mother says, and maybe this is what makes me feel like trying again.

"Who wants to come to the beach with me?" I ask. "Agnes? Mom?"

"I'm going to drive to town," Agnes says.

"No, thanks," my mother says, glancing at the boardwalk and away, slipping her sunglasses on. "You go ahead."

I have this sense that she is afraid, like if I can get her to go, she'll be happy. "Come on, Mom," I say. "A little walk. Ten minutes."

"I said no," she says flatly.

I walk to the ocean alone, take off my sandals, and roll my pants cuffs, tread in the surf. The late afternoon crowd has thinned, and the low sun glints on the water. The waves fizz over the sand, sting, recede. I wish my mother were here. The happiest I've seen her in a long time is when she was planning the trip, anticipating the whole thing. Maybe the crowds are too much for her, I think. Or maybe she wants to go alone. But tomorrow? If we found a more isolated beach?

For months before I'd ended things with Javi, I'd felt that my life was not real; in an irrational but deep, instinctual way, I felt that if I did not get married, did not have children, if I held my breath, time would not pass and I would not age and the things that mattered to me would not fall away. But we can't save ourselves. Her house on the hill by the sea, I think: surely she knows she will never get it. Doesn't she want to see the ocean for these few days, while she can, while she's spending this money she can't afford to spend? What is she saving it for? Waiting, I think: we do it too well.

Dark is falling as I get back to the Sea Latch, feet sandy and goose pimples rising on my calves, and stop in the lobby / coffee shop to see about getting a cup of tea. The clerk hasn't yet turned on the lights, and the place looks deserted, the linoleum sunk in shadow, the ancient, plastic-ridged price board over the pastry counter almost unreadable. A silver bell sits on the lobby desk. I ring it and wait, shifting uncomfortably, the wet bottoms of my jeans heavy and stiffening. The high, pure note of the bell sounds, wavers, and dies. I ring the bell again. A gray-haired woman emerges from the back. Her thick hair rolls away from her face in pretty waves, and her lower lip protrudes, covering an overbite. The effect is to give her a slight pout.

She hits the overhead lights, and the fluorescent tubes flicker and buzz before snapping on. "What can I do for you?"

She looks, in the darkness before the lights make her ordinary, like the girl from the morning, grown old over the course of the day, her spine curving and skin wrinkling, her pale hair darkening to silver. Her face shifting. Her teeth. Teeth: the one part of the skeleton that shows, the one part we would know each other by if our skin and muscle and tendons and blood dropped away and we stood before each other, saying, It's me. Do you remember me?

"Miss?" she says.

"Do you have herbal tea?" I ask. "Without caffeine? I've been having a tough time sleeping."

She heats water in a Styrofoam cup and retrieves a teabag from the back, waving away my two quarters. I drop the quarters in the tip jar. She is bent over the pastry case, shifting muffins. At the sound, she smiles and nods to herself privately.

"Thanks," I call, as I let myself out. Twenty minutes—maybe my mother would be willing to go that far. We've already come three hours, crossed state lines.

"Good luck," she replies. She means falling asleep, but it gives me a jolt. It is as if in sliding open the door to that dusty glass case, she's reached her hand into my thoughts.

Dusk has fallen. Blowing on my tea, I sip the warm water against the evening's chill. From the carpeted porch outside our motel room, I look back at the lobby. Lit up, the small interior seems warm and welcoming, a beacon in the darkening parking lot, and casts a ring of light on the pavement. I think of a game I played as a girl on car rides, where I'd pretend I could lift the car as it skimmed the pavement. I would lift the car with my mind so it wouldn't touch shadow, set it back down once we reached sunlight. The more sunlight the tires touched, the better. The game had no real end.

Two pairs of flip-flops sit outside the motel room, but the room itself is empty. Agnes isn't back yet. My mother is taking a shower. When she comes out, toweling her hair, she's changed into sweatpants, a sign she's in for the night.

"Did you make it to the ocean today?" I ask.

"Not today," she says.

Agnes comes in, carrying a stuffed sea lion she's bought in town for the baby.

"Agnes, look," I say, taking the slick tourist map from my straw bag. She approaches, tentatively. I unfold the map. "The woman at the motel said there's a less crowded beach not far from here. It's gorgeous, she says. I was thinking about checking it out. We could go tomorrow, swim, lie out. You'd love it, I bet."

"Maybe," Agnes says.

"What about you, Mom?"

"I think I want to go to the pool," she says.

"The woman said it's beautiful," I say.

"We'll see," she says. Her tone is even, but final. But a little later she asks how long I'd said it took to get to the beach and whether it was crowded and what the sand was like.

I get up early the next day—our last full day at the Sea Latch—and walk to a convenience store to buy a better area map. The tourist map lacks detail, and I don't want to get lost and watch my mother grow uneasy and go quiet, stare out the passenger-side car window like we might never get home. In blue ink, I star the motel and Old Orchard Beach, connect them with a firm line. When my mother and Agnes awaken, I ask who wants to come.

"It sounds pretty," Agnes says, and looks at my mother, but my mother says no. She says she might take a walk on York Beach that afternoon to see the ocean.

"You go if you want," she says. "I won't need the car."

I think of the sandy white beaches, of the motel pool. My mother digs in her purse and produces the car key. "No, thanks," I say.

"In case you change your mind," she says, laying the key on the nightstand.

When she and Agnes leave for the pool, I say, "I'll catch up with you later."

I change into my bathing suit and, taking the car key with me, go to the coffee shop, buy a stale biscotti and coffee, and skim the local newspaper. BIDDEFORD TO ALTER WASTE FEES. SWEET EMOTIONS AT YORK FATHER-DAUGHTER DANCE. GOLDEN TROJANS: LIGHTING IT UP WHEN IT COUNTS. After breakfast I get in the car. Then I get back out, go to the motel room, replace the key, and walk across the parking lot to the pool.

My mother lies on her lounge chair. She shields her eyes with a hand, squinting as if in pain. "Sun keeps moving," she says, and stands to move her chair. I go to help, too late. "I've got it," she says. Chair arranged, she lies back and shuts her eyes. She doesn't look happy, but she doesn't look unhappy, either. She looks like she usually does.

Agnes and I swim. Agnes gets out after a while and dries her hair. She tilts her head, bangs lightly on her temple with the heel of her hand. In profile, standing with her back arched, her stomach looks flat. "Do you care what it is?" I ask.

"Water in my ear," she says to my mother. "Again." Then, "No, not really." After a pause, she says, "What do you want it to be?"

"The kind of baby that lets you stay in college," I say.

She laughs. My mother doesn't.

"Agnes'll be close to home," she says. "She can stay in college if she wants to. People do it all the time."

My mother dropped out after her first semester to marry our father. About my sister's college prospects, she's often said, "She's not a very good reader."

"Yeah, but having a baby makes it harder," I say.

"I'm going for a walk," my mother announces, standing and folding her towel. "I'll be back soon."

"Where are you going?" I ask.

"The boardwalk."

"I'll go with you," Agnes offers.

"I will too," I say. They want to be alone. I know it, but I don't care. I am hungry and irritable. I am tired of feeling left out, and I am tired of sitting in a parking lot.

My mother looks at me, then at Agnes, applying her lip gloss, which she says is SPF 15. "You don't both need to come," she says. "Isn't it time for one of your regular meals?"

"I'm okay," I say. I slide one wet foot into a flip-flop, then the other, pull my sundress over my head, collect my towel. "Ready."

My mother shrugs. She puts on her sweatpants and an oversized T-shirt. Agnes finger-combs her hair, readjusts her bikini, pulling the waistband up so the little bulge in her stomach isn't visible, tugging the halter top's underwire into place so that her breasts, which were always bigger than you'd expect for her frame and have become a cup size larger since she got pregnant, are offered up like pale poached eggs in twin peach egg holders.

"Do you think I should go back to the room and get a cover-up?" Agnes asks me.

"Nah," I say, because she clearly doesn't want to and because I know it'll annoy my mother.

My mother eyes Agnes's breasts. "It'll be chillier by the water," she says. "You might bring a sweatshirt."

"I'll be okay," Agnes says.

At the boardwalk, my mother looks panicked. The walkway is crowded. To get onto it you have to find a gap between adults lugging canvas tote bags, boogie boards, and plastic pails of beach toys and kids chasing each other and yelling, weaving in and out, their sandy feet flying with a thud-thud over the wood. Bottlenecks form around food vendors. She stands frozen for a minute, unsure of what direction to go. Seagulls congregate in front of us, fighting over a hamburger bun. She glances at Agnes, who doesn't see the look because she is busy checking out a lifeguard who stands on the top rungs of his white wooden chair, blowing his whistle. My mother takes a hesitant step forward, but the gulls ignore this and keep pecking and calling, and she stops, waits for us to go first. I feel bad for having wanted to annoy her.

The small strip of gray sand is spotted with beach towels. The tide has come almost to the boardwalk and is now ebbing. The sand is still wet, so the beach isn't covered with people. The locals are at York's private beaches, and many of the out-of-towners have probably driven the twenty minutes to Old Orchard Beach, with its wide expanse of fine white sand.

"Let's walk down to the water," I say. "It's less crowded."

Agnes leads the way, taking us past the lifeguard's chair. Men watch her as she walks. I can tell she notices, though she doesn't return their glances. Her legs are long and tanned, her thighs paler than her calves. She walks lightly, bouncing on the balls of her feet. She could be any girl I knew from Williams. You can't tell she's pregnant.

My mother tends to walk slowly because her medication makes her sluggish, but today she walks even more slowly than normal. She pauses to remove her sandals as we near the ocean. The distance between us and Agnes grows.

"I don't want you bothering her about being pregnant," my mother says, when Agnes is out of earshot.

"I haven't been," I say.

"Well, good. Keep it up."

"The time to bother her would've been before she got pregnant."

"Meaning what?" my mother says. She stops. Her T-shirt sleeves hang almost to her elbows, and she pushes them up angrily. "Meaning I should've kept this from happening?"

That is what I meant. Thinking of her frozen on the boardwalk, though, I don't see how. How could I expect her to stop anything when she can barely bring herself to leave the house?

"Meaning nothing."

I start to walk on. She doesn't move. "Come on, Mom," I say.

"No," she says. "I've had enough." She moves away from the water's edge. Once the tide can't reach her, she stops. She crouches again and puts her sandals back on. Without looking at me, she begins to walk back toward the motel.

"Mom," I call after her. She doesn't turn. I watch her approach the boardwalk. She flinches when she reaches the crowd of beachgoers, hovers at the walkway's edge in the way of a person who knows no one at a party. She looks small, lost. I will her to turn back, but she doesn't. Hesitatingly, she steps into the crowd. I see her freeze, and the swim-suited throngs close around her like water around a buoy. Then she begins to move forward, carried on the eddies until she is gone.

I sit down on the beach. The sand's wetness seeps through my sundress, and, miserable and angry, I look around for what I can throw. The beach is picked clean of driftwood and shells, so I take off my flip-flops and chuck them into the ocean, one after the other. The second one floats on a cresting wave, bobbing along before being sucked under when the wave breaks. Thinking about the walk back to the motel without shoes, I feel worse.

Agnes is a quarter-mile up the coast, talking to two boys in long swim trunks, both holding surfboards. I catch up with her as the better-looking one, taller, with blond-streaked hair, is describing a drinking game called Das Boot. He mimics the way you hold the boot, his hands in the air, head thrown back as he chugs the imaginary beer. Agnes giggles. The other boy takes the opportunity to watch her breasts. He holds his surfboard stiffly, planted at his feet like a shield. A white shell necklace glints around his neck.

The boys size me up as I approach. When Agnes turns and smiles at me, the taller one's face grows hopeful and then, when I fail to make eye contact with him, surly. In that moment, I am almost happy Agnes is pregnant, since this means he has no real chance with her. At least I hope it means that.

"Hey," Agnes says, more agreeable than normal for her audience's sake. "Where's Mom?"

"Back at the motel," I say.

"Why?" Agnes asks. Concern shows on her face.

"She was tired," I say.

"And she went back by herself?"

"Yeah."

The blond boy jogs up the beach to his towel. He rummages around and trots back to us, holding aloft a cell phone. His shoulders are peeling from sunburn, the edges of the dead skin translucent. "Agnes, we'll call you if we go to that clam shack," he says. He keys her name into the phone and hands it to her. She types in her number, frowning with concentration, hits Save, and passes the phone back to him.

The boys leave. "Let's get lunch," I say. Agnes turns toward the food stands. "No, at the hotel."

She looks dubious. "Can I go in my bathing suit?"

I hand her my sweatshirt. She puts it on.

At a tourist stand I stop and buy a new pair of sandals for me and a sarong for Agnes. "Here," I say. "A skirt." I show her how to wrap the fabric and tie it at her hip.

We walk to the edge of the beach. The white hotel is quieter in the daylight, nice but less grand looking. The hostess asks whether we want to sit inside or on the deck. I look at Agnes, waiting for her to express an opinion. She glances inside, at the dining room's chandeliers and dark wood. "The deck," she says.

I order linguine and clams. Agnes gets a BLT.

We eat in silence, watching the waves break against the rocks. Finally, I say, "So how are you feeling about the baby?"

"Okay," she says. She picks at the crinkly yellow plastic on the toothpick that held the BLT together. "You know. Excited, I guess."

I wait.

She sighs. "I know once the baby's born, I won't feel like I'm missing out on stuff, but right now I kind of do."

"So why didn't you tell me when you found out?"

Agnes stops shredding the plastic. She looks past me, at a fishing boat bobbing near the horizon. "I didn't want you to talk me out of it."

On the walk back to the Sea Latch, Agnes is quiet. Once, she asks about the month Javi and I had planned to spend at his aunt's apartment in Madrid. We cancelled our tickets when we broke up. Agnes says I should go anyway. I tell her I can't afford it; giving up a month's research time would've been hard, and paying to rent an apartment in Madrid on top of that is out of the question. "Maybe someday I can pay for you to go," she says. "Yeah?" I say. "When you're rich?" "When I'm rich," she says with a grin that reminds me of the way she used to smile at me when her line passed mine in the halls of our elementary school, her kindergarten class headed in a rowdy row to gym, my seventh-grade class slouching along on the way to art. "I hear kidneys fetch a good price on the black market," I say. She gives a surprised laugh, a short, choked sound that catches in her throat. "Babies, too," she says.

"Two problems solved at once," I say, then, quickly, "Not that your baby is a problem."

"Yeah," she says. "I know."

Our motel room is empty. We check the grounds. The pool is empty; the buoys separating the shallow end from the deep end bob in a melancholy rhythm. Our car is in the parking lot, unmoved. The Sea Latch coffee shop closed at two, and the woman working the lobby desk says she hasn't seen our mother. "Maybe she went to eat," I say, feeling the unlikeliness as I speak. Agnes shakes her head.

We leave a note and take the car. Traffic on Route 1 crawls past the beach, cars pausing every fifty feet for swimmers in the crosswalks. I drive, and Agnes puts on her sunglasses and lowers the window, scanning the boardwalk and the little strip of beach. While we're stopped at a crosswalk, Agnes says, "I scheduled an abortion. But then I got there, and they asked what the appointment was for, and I couldn't say. So I walked out."

"When was this?"

"Before I told anybody. Then I told Tully and he was so excited and Mom was too, and I started thinking maybe I did want to have the baby. And now I know I do."

"Are you sure?"

"Yeah," she said. She leans her head out the window. The wind whips her hair away from her face, twisting it into ropey sections that will later hang thick and snarled like seaweed. "Don't ever tell Mom I wasn't, okay?"

"Okay," I say.

We drive around town for an hour but don't find our mother. When we get back to the Sea Latch, she is washing sand from her feet in the bathtub.

"Where'd you go?" Agnes asks.

"The beach," she says. "Same as you."

We eat dinner that night at a restaurant near the motel. I pay, in a belated celebration of Agnes's pregnancy. As a concession to me, my mother orders steak, though she only eats a bite. Agnes gets fries and an ice cream sundae. "What?" she says defensively when I give her a look. "The doctor said I should get lots of dairy." She says she's decided to name the baby after my mother. The baby's middle name will be Teresa if it's a girl, or Briggs, my mother's maiden name, if it's a boy.

My mother and Agnes go outside to have a cigarette. I pay the bill and get a box for my mother's food so she can eat it later on tonight, when she gets hungry.

Agnes and my mother settle in at the motel after dinner, and I leave to go for a drive by myself. To watch the Red Sox game, I say, but really, I just feel lonely. I hope being alone will make the loneliness invisible, like hanging a white canvas on a white wall. After following the coastal highway a few miles, I turn off, drive aimlessly until my eyes feel gritty. Driving back to the Sea Latch, I get lost. The highway looks different in the moonlight. I end up by a stretch of beach I haven't seen before. The road runs alongside a high, rocky embankment that drops steeply to the water. I pull over and get out of the car. The temperature has plunged dramatically, and a cold wind is coming off the water—the air feels forty-five, maybe fifty—and I am still wearing the sundress I put on this afternoon. My mother has left a pair of sweatpants in the car, and I pull them on under my dress and leave the car by the side of the road as I walk to the edge of the rocks to see the ocean.

A rocky ledge juts over the water. The waves are far below. I think of the house my mother had wanted.

There in the dark, the ocean pulls at me. An urge to throw myself off the rocks into the water begins to form in my chest, solidifying and then tugging, like a string connecting me to the waves. It doesn't feel like a wish to escape, but like a terrible curiosity, similar to the desire to read a loved one's journal. The feeling has no traceable origin—I don't want to hurt myself—and no logic, but the impulse is physical, like a reflex, and that makes it scarier. It feels as if my body could make a choice without my authorizing it. I step back from the rocks. Sitting down on the cold, damp sand, I close my eyes and listen. I can feel myself dropping further inside myself. I stay there until my fingers go numb. I have to warm the engine and blow hot air on them before driving.

The parking lot is quiet. The lobby's dark windows reflect the string of white lights by the motel pool. The lights are roped around the trunks of trees, outlining their branches, like you might see outside fancy establishments in Los Angeles.

Walking by the pool, I stop and press my face against the chain-link fence. The metal is cold against my skin. The lifeguard chair is empty. An abandoned round foam life preserver floats in the pool, as though the lifeguard has vanished while attempting a rescue. A gust of wind slaps the water, and the foam circle spins and drifts, its cheerful stripes giving it a toylike appearance. It reminds me of the pendants used by hypnotists on TV.

I wonder what is inside my mother that makes her so scared. I wonder what is inside me. I feel like I may never know.

My mother and Agnes are asleep. Agnes shifts when I let myself in, mutters an indistinguishable word, sinks back into dream. My mother doesn't move.

We check out at 11:00 a.m. Before turning away from the coast, my mother slows the car and rolls down her window. The strong light makes the lines on her face less noticeable and softens her hair, which she colors from a Clairol box several shades too dark—her one act of defiance against aging. She looks a little like I remember her from childhood, when I thought she was so beautiful.

She smiles at us, closes her eyes, and inhales.

"Breathe deep, girls," she says. "That's the ocean."

At the Wrong Time, to the Wrong People

SHE AND HER SISTER work together silently. They no longer need to speak. They focus on the dog, moving him as they would a mattress. Half collie, half German shepherd, he weighs a good eighty pounds. Together, they prop his forelegs on the stairs that lead to the second floor of the house. He whines softly as they raise his legs so that his body stretches toward the sky.

Teresa holds the dog's bowl to his mouth. Seven. This is the seventh day that he has not been able to eat properly, that his esophagus has refused to function, that she and her sister have needed to hold him in such a way that gravity pulls the food from his throat to his stomach, so that he starves more slowly than he would otherwise. A rich, meaty smell rises from the dish she holds to his nose. The dog laps weakly, pants, grins at her.

Given his choice, the dog would have stopped eating days ago, would have let his weakness numb him, carry him off somewhere she can't follow: into unconsciousness and then death. Death: she can name it, but he can't, and she wonders, briefly, at the propriety of getting this dog to defend against her ex-husband, even to death, and then to refuse to relinquish him when nature attempts what violence has not.

"They don't feel pain as we do," the vet said once. What he meant, surely, was that the dog cannot think self-reflexively, cannot wonder what he would do if an intruder was to enter, whose life he would prefer to sacrifice—hers, her ex-husband's, their daughters', his own—and which second, which third, which fourth, which last—that lying awake wondering this cannot be a source of pain for a dog. But then a dog also cannot grow accustomed to pain, cannot come to greet it as a tolerable, if contemptible, dinner guest. Each time she feeds the dog this way, hurting him no matter how gently she hefts his skinny ribcage onto the carpeted stair, how much of his weight she supports with her own body, he casts his watery eyes on her with a look that says, I did not expect this from you.

When the dog finishes eating, tired—he rests his muzzle on the bowl, leaving half the portion of mushy food to congeal beneath his nose, as he would not have done even yesterday, even this morning—she and her sister ease him off the stairs. He limps to the window, circles three times, and plops with a sigh onto an old wool blanket she has spread for him. The dog carries himself with dignity, but no longer with grace; lying down is now a process of positioning himself over the spot where he will rest and letting go. She had thought to use her goose-down comforter—he deserved that, at least—but then she could not afford a new one, and the dog does not know the difference between one softness and another.

She shifts her weight from her sore right hip to her left, considering. Outside, a maple tree, brilliant in the furious blush of fall, rustles. A shadow moves across the dog's tail, retreats. Sunlight draws a horseshoe on his lank fur.

She can put off his death another day, if she wishes. Even two. This, she can choose. But choose she must, and not between fates but between hours. So after her sister leaves, taking the girls for milkshakes and a sleepover, each pausing to kiss the dog, once, twice, again, their long, dark hair brushing the blanket as they nuzzle his neck and stroke his chest, when the house is quiet, she calls the vet, asks him to come. And later that afternoon, he does.

From the kitchen, she hears his truck crunching up the gravel driveway. He is a big man, handsome. She stands by the window, just out of sight, and watches his approach. His mouth is puckered as if she might greet him with a kiss, and as he gets closer, she sees he is whistling. Climbing the wooden steps her ex-husband built, he hesitates, steps back down them, stoops, and examines the soft places. She has noticed the beginnings of rot, has taken a book out from the public library on the subject of home repair, but this is a project she is saving for when she can sleep again. She doesn't trust herself with a chain saw otherwise.

She is at the door before he knocks.

"Thanks for being willing to come out here, especially on a Sunday," she says.

She lives on a dirt road, remote, far from his clinic, which is also his home; he keeps a small apartment on the second floor.

The vet smiles, shrugs. "Wasn't doing much anyways. Just puttering around."

She shows him into the living room.

"Do it here or outside?" he asks.

"Here," she says.

He asks if she will stay with the dog, and she says, "Yes."

She crouches down. The dog, sensing her pain, is disturbed. He licks her face in anxious anticipation. The vet unpacks his equipment, frowning at the needle he flicks to settle the liquid inside. She sits. The dog uses his front legs to pull his body forward until he is half in her lap.

"Good boy," she says. She strokes his soft ears, feeling the give of the cartilage as she pulls them back the way he likes her to, trying to usher this creature out of his brief flicker of consciousness with the same quality of attention to his comfort that he has always, easily, given her. But she fails, can think only of herself. The vet finds his vein, and the dog yelps, goes rigid, then slackens, his eyes still fixed on her, worried. Still asking her, What is it? What's hurting you?

Of course she knows that the vet will take the dog's body away; she has asked him to. But when he says, "Ready?" she doesn't know what he means. She nods anyway, only realizes when he lifts the dog in his arms in one quick motion. As she stands, the vet hefts the dog to redistribute the weight. The dog's body shifts and settles with the loose heaviness of a sack of mulch.

"Thank you," she says. She isn't sure who she's thanking, or for what.

She opens the front door for the vet.

"Time to go home, old boy," the vet says, addressing the dog. "We'll send the bill," he says to her.

"Thank you," she says again.

Watching the vet carry the dog to his truck, she thinks the worst is over, for this afternoon at least. But then the vet stops, and the dog's mouth opens and a clear liquid pours out onto the ground. She can see the dirt darken. The vet waits until there is no more, and then carries the dog the rest of the way to his pickup. He throws the dog's body in the back.

"Wait," she calls from the door.

She goes upstairs and returns with her goose-down. As she carries it to the truck, she thinks, I am a foolish woman.

"Do you mind?" she asks. The vet shakes his head. He stands back, lets her tuck the blanket around the dog. The dog's legs are splayed unnaturally, as though he has slipped on a wet floor. His body is no longer his own. When she secures the blanket's edges around his hips, his hindquarters don't respond to her touch.

I have given everything at the wrong time, to the wrong people, she thinks.

Tomorrow, when her girls come home, she will tell them that the dog is gone. They will be angry she didn't tell them before, so they could say goodbye. The oldest will chew her hair, the youngest may hit her, as she did after she told the girls they wouldn't be seeing their father for a while. "What did you do?" she asked. "What did you do to him?" But that's tomorrow. Now she is alone, and she must thaw the chicken for dinner and wash the old blanket where an hour ago the dog lay so that when twilight comes creeping into the house, dragging the night chill behind, she will be safe.

She punches the security code into the alarm, arming it. She rinses the dog's bowl in the sink. She runs the water until it is warm, holds her hands underneath. She turns on lights as she enters rooms, turns them off as she leaves. She pulls the curtains closed against the darkness.

Shoulder Season

MY WEEK HAD been quiet. It was March, not cool, but not hot, and everything getting ready to bloom. Saguaros, green and erect, stretching up from the dun-colored desert. No other houses in sight. His nearest neighbor, a mile down the road. The first day, I had seen a rattlesnake. I'd called the dogs back just in time. It took me a few minutes to stop shaking. The night before this, my ex-boyfriend had emailed me. Not Javier, not Michael, but the person for whom I had once lain awake all night, unable to sleep, and eventually walked myself to the hospital, saying that I thought I was losing my mind. I'd waited in a cold room in a robe, crying, for an hour. No one came. Eventually, they let me leave.

He had dreamed about me, he wrote, and he missed me still. In two months, he was getting married.

That last part, he didn't tell me; that, I knew from looking him up online.

His fiancée had registered for plain white towels.

The first time he kissed me, I was twenty-one. He looked so vulnerable, so given over to happiness. So—I don't know how else to say this—so mortal.

Who needed that? Not me.

I deleted the email. Then I deleted the deleted copy. Then I spent an hour trying to get it back.

On Sunday afternoon, I stood on the roof deck. The deck overlooked a wild, beautiful stretch of Sonoran desert. Coming from the Northeast, the landscape awed me still: purple mountains and vast sky and undulating waves of light, dry earth. Beside me, my advisor stood, drinking a beer. An hour earlier, he had arrived home from the airport. He had been staying in Berlin for the past week with his new love, a German physicist named Johannes whom he'd met in Amsterdam, while I looked after his dogs.

I hadn't planned to tell him about my decision, not yet, but we'd been talking about love, new love, and, though it was a radical thing to say and an even more radical thing to do, the truth had emerged from my mouth: I was done. I was quitting the program. Now, we were looking at each other, surprised.

"But why?" he asked me.

"A job offer," he said. "You've accepted an offer."

"No."

"Then what?"

Before I could answer, he said, "You won't have to move somewhere you'll hate, somewhere without men. Not if you don't want to be an academic, and you don't need to be."

"It's not that."

"It's Javier."

"No."

"You're two years away. Maybe one."

A jet flew by, marking the sky with the faint white lines my neighbor Miles called weeping chemical trails. He had studied classics at Harvard in the seventies. Now he was in his sixties. He was tall and rangy, athletic. Though he was HIV-positive, he'd been able to manage the illness. His gentleness and intelligence were evident when he spoke, though he also had some strange ideas. He lived behind my house in a little studio, taking care of small repairs for the woman who owned the buildings. In his spare time he kept up his Latin and Greek.

"Don't do it," my advisor said. "Don't give this up for nothing."

I was writing back then, had just started, and I was trying to write myself out of a rage I didn't want or understand.

"I won't," I said.

He looked relieved, but that wasn't what I meant.

The day before I'd begun to write, I went by Sylvie's place. "It is too hot to live," Sylvie said in greeting, her hair wet from a cool afternoon shower. I envied her nonchalance and her legs, which were long and golden brown and tapered to elegant ankles with little divots on either side of the long bone. The heat was making everyone insane, people were not supposed to live in the desert, Sylvie continued, she was leaving the desert, she was moving to San Diego, that was it, she was moving to the beach, it was final. But then she emerged from the bathroom wearing a faded green bikini and we set up lawn chairs in her sandy yard and drank cheap white wine with ice cubes and invited the sun to bake our brains into a fine casserole.

We were neighbors, more or less. She lived four blocks away in a casita behind a large wooden fence with a metal gate she would prop open for me on Sunday nights when I came over to join her to watch bad programming on her small TV set. People in our neighborhood liked fences, or, to say it another way, they didn't like meth addicts breaking in. Three times that year Sylvie's car windows had been smashed, and it was only April.

Now it was the shoulder season of the day: late afternoon, a pause. We sat in the sun. Sylvie yawned; I scratched my leg. What I wanted most was for us to go on this way: all potential, no action. I liked this state. Longing was, I felt, preferable to disappointment.

"What if your soulmate and your best friend and the love of your life turn out to be three different people?" she asked me.

"It's a stupid question," she said, "but this guy asked me, and now I can't stop thinking about it."

"I'd be pleased if I met one of them."

"What if one turns out to be a really bad person," she said, "like a murderer, or one of those people who insists on correcting other people's pronunciation?"

"It's said, 'eh-pit-oh-me,'" I said.

Nothing was turning out as we had imagined, and maybe it was the strength of the desert sun, but we felt like we were squinting toward a future that glowed white without possessing any discernible shape. Waking and looking out the window, I sometimes could not recall whether it was January or July. This dislocation felt pleasantly cottonlike, like waking from anesthesia and drifting back to a sweet, drugged sleep.

"I hope one's a dog," I said.

When my intentions became clear, my advisor said: "I should have known."

"Why?" I asked.

"You didn't come to Boston."

"It wasn't because I was thinking about quitting," I said, but then I thought about it more and maybe it was. It was that year, in his absence, that I had seen how work might become a sort of obliteration, how I might dedicate myself to answering questions that grew smaller and smaller until I myself could not remember why I was asking them, could not, some days, engage with them as anything other than ritual, and while I saw the point, of course I saw the point, I could not help but think of a story I had read in college in which it was said of a person,

"What stood out about him was that his life got put past him." And then I went to Sylvie's, and then I began; and now, eleven months later, here we were on his roof deck, saying goodbye.

What made me decide? To be honest, I don't know. It was like waking up from that sweet, drugged sleep and feeling panic that it had all been real after all. No one had told me. I had just been supposed to know. It didn't go well at first, and that was a relief. I'm not going to do this, I thought. But then I didn't stop. It was a bit like falling in love. Much harder, but as helpless-making.

Your face: the thing I loved best. The thing I watched doors for.

A salt-rim moon. A dry, rustling wind.

One of the most shocking things, I would come to find, was how easily my life dropped away.

At home, I went to bed alone. According to his new love, my advisor had told me that afternoon, Germans don't interrupt each other the way Americans do. In German, the verb comes at the end, so Germans have to hear each other out to discover what the action will be. "Do you believe him?" I asked. "Not really," he said. "But I don't interrupt him anymore either."

When I had broken up with Javier, my advisor had told me, "Don't worry. Life keeps giving you chances." "Chances to what?" I'd asked. "Chances to love things," he'd said. "Chances to become someone new." I knew that didn't happen, of course; only romantics thought so.

Still, I wanted a chance to love something. I wanted a chance to become someone new.

·III·

Metaphor

HE SAID, "The house we argued in front of yesterday burned to the ground." She laughed, shook her head. It felt true. It felt like a metaphor for their entire relationship. "No," he said. "I mean it. Walk by. There's nothing there anymore."

Vision

I WAS STAYING in Virginia for seventeen days that spring at an artists' residency. The dorm building in which we were housed was a seventies-style structure with small, monastic rooms and shared bathrooms. The other artists were mostly middle-aged women; one hung up a plea for quiet in the morning, another for quiet in the evening, and I walked around gingerly, trying not to make noise. At thirty-two, I was the second-youngest in residence, the youngest being a dark-blonde-haired girl from Washington, DC, whose boyfriend lived in South Africa and who went on long runs by herself in the late afternoons. Our rooms shared a bathroom, and we struck up a friendship right away.

By the end of my third day, I had met almost everyone, except for one old man. On his face he affixed white surgical tape. The two half-inch strips began above the arcs of his bushy gray eyebrows and ran up the middle of his forehead, giving him a perpetually surprised look. This odd fact, and his lonerish quality, made him a figure of interest.

Mornings, he stomped glumly around the blushing green grounds, taciturn and anonymous. I would spot him from my window as I prepared to walk the quarter mile to my studio—our studios were separate from our living quarters—and each night he would pass me on the staircase in silence, failing to reply to my soft "Good evening," a ghost with a limp and a cane.

Late in the evening of my third day, I asked a few others about him.

"Who, the old guy?" said Aaron, who occupied the studio across from mine. "He's a painter, but I understand he has vision trouble."

Sophie, the girl from Washington, DC, sat with us. We were drinking cheap wine in a windowless room shaped like a silo.

"Do you know anything about him?" Aaron asked her.

She shook her head, curls bouncing. "He never talks."

But when I entered breakfast after an early walk the next morning, the old painter approached my table.

"Is this seat taken?" he asked me, leaning on his cane, and I said, "Please."

He carried a cup of coffee, which he set on the table, sloshing a bit into the saucer.

"What do you do?" he said. "I'm a writer," I replied. "And what are you working on?" he asked, shakily lowering himself to his chair. When I deflected, not feeling up to discussing my latest efforts, the dismal results of which made me worry that I had been wrong to quit my doctoral program, he began to tell me about his situation: he was going blind. He had lost seventy percent of his vision. He wasn't sure how he was still painting, but he was. It sounded like a tough situation, I said, and asked him how he liked Virginia, trying to distract him from his obvious misery. This, however, was not a happier topic. He praised the countryside's beauty and quietness and said he wanted to leave the city, but he couldn't. He had been born there and he lived there and he could not escape.

"New York keeps sucking me in like a vortex."

"You can't leave?" I asked.

"No. I would be much happier in the countryside."

"So why not move? Surely there's a way."

"My vision. Driving would be necessary in the country. But I'm still painting. I don't know how but I am."

"How do you know if they're any good?"

He smiled, his expression wry. "Other people tell me."

". . . I'm joking mostly," he added. "Natural light helps. In strong natural light, I can see a bit. That's why I have the studio with all the windows. Twelve o'clock is best."

As I finished my oatmeal, he extended a hand. His fingers were strong and blunt, the nail beds oddly flat. "David," he said. "Nice talking," I said, and rose to go to work, leaving him sitting there with his weak, milky cup of coffee, gazing out the window at whatever it was he could still see.

But the words would not come. Each day, I sat alone in my studio in silence. One morning, I typed the first things that came into my head, and erased them. They were glib. Instead, I read. On small index cards, I copied out the words of others and hung these cards around my studio like small prayers.

One card read:

> Her English-speaking voice is misleading: hesitant and lilting with the nervous charm of someone who is new to a language.

A second card read:

> It's like being in a tunnel. Finally I emerge onto the brilliance of the *quai*, beneath a roof of glass panels which seems to magnify the light.

A third card read:

—the frightening gills,
fresh and crisp with blood,
that can cut so badly—
I thought of the coarse white flesh
packed in like feathers,
the big bones and the little bones

A fourth card read:

That April I felt so heavy and I went to the sauna to feel less heavy but it didn't work. I went because I wanted to remember that the heart was a muscle more than it was a metaphor: when it hurt the hurt was most often a metaphor, but when the hot-cold-hot of my rotation from sauna to ice bath and back made it thump crazily against my ribs, that pounding was the muscle laboring to keep me alive.

To do this I sat in the late March sunlight at my borrowed wooden desk, whose drawers smelled of mouse urine, as is the tendency of old furniture in warm climates, and used a thick, black-inked artist's pen. The casing was a soft gray, of German manufacture. On its top it read 0.3. I was no artist; I had bought the pen because I liked its heft. The heavy nib exerted resistance when I guided it over the paper. I did this with care, like a person using an axe to tap a nail into a wall. It felt good to employ a tool I could not reasonably be expected to wield with any facility, to put this tool to work on an achievable task. The small white notecards I posted on the wall with silver thumbtacks.

My studio contained three windows, a twin-sized bed, and a flight of stairs that led down from a raised landing to the main floor. Outside, horses grazed. When I wasn't copying out passages, I sat by a window with a view of the pasture, reading or just looking at the brighter world outside.

· · ·

The old painter was talking about painting. You had to know when to stop, that was the hard thing. Many young painters did not know and they ruined their work.

"*Iberpotshke* is Yiddish for *overwork*," he was saying. "A beautiful, onomatopoeic word. And *iber* means *over*, so *iber*-iberpotshke is *over*-overworked."

"So how do you know when to stop?" I asked.

"Practice. Years and years. And confidence: you must have confidence."

His left eye bulged, pale-blue, sightless. His faded chambray shirt was unbuttoned halfway down his chest in the style of the seventies, white chest hair showing. Tiny, bright paint flecks of every color speckled the fabric.

It was 6 p.m. We moved into the dining room. I got in line and began chatting with a few women; he stopped to examine the chalkboard menu, though I doubted he could read it. Sitting down, I forgot about him. For dinner that night, the chef had made a bright sautéed kale and tough dried-out pork. The meat came apart in desiccated strips, white flesh clinging and fibrous. I had spent the day staring at the pages of a novel I'd written the previous year, a terrible novel. What made the words so bad? It was not each word on its own. Recombined, they might be okay. Some phrases I even liked. On the sentence level, though, the words became attenuated, uninspired. Not terrible, but mundane. It was when the sentences piled on each other like logs making a hut that the thing became truly awful. This was, I imagined, like painting: you added color after color and you created an ugly brown.

I imagined torching the hut.

"I'm a good cook," the old painter said at my elbow.

He had found me and sat beside me, though normally he ate alone in silence. Now, each time I spoke to the woman on my other side, he butted in like a recalcitrant goat.

"What do you like to cook?" I asked him politely.

"Italian, though I'm not." He paused. "But I don't like to follow a recipe," he continued. "I don't bake. I'm an abstract expressionist in the kitchen. I can go to a restaurant and eat a dish and know how to make it. I cooked better than all my girlfriends. They would go to my cooking school and go off and cook for another man."

We shared a table with five women, all much older than me. By some fluke most people in residence were in their fifties or sixties, which had made me feel close to Sophie and Aaron immediately. One woman, a German woman seated across from me, was truly old. She dyed her hair jet black and wore it bobbed, a little cap.

"So you never married?" I asked.

"No," he said.

"Do you have children?"

"No, fortunately or unfortunately. I consider it unfortunate."

He frowned, his browned, mottled face a pinch.

"The kale," said a female printmaker from the Cape, returning to the table. She lived now in London with her husband, a banker, who funded her art-making. "I've found out the secret. Cook it with garlic and a little olive oil and cumin and add salt and lemon juice toward the end." She was bossy, self-promotional. Her studio in London, she liked to complain, was poorly heated. She could walk there from her apartment but the route was not pretty; it was industrial.

"But that's *his* recipe," a middle-aged Dutch sculptor named Ilse exclaimed, meaning the old painter, who had correctly guessed the kale's ingredients while the printmaker was away from the table. "But exactly!"

The old painter said nothing, smiled privately.

The printmaker was not impressed. The look on her face told us so. She didn't like his complaints, having, perhaps, a life too full of complaint herself, and was not interested in what he had to say. He, however, could not see this. "Wow," she said flatly. "Imagine that." He muttered a modest "Well, yes, it's always been a talent," and excused himself, triumphant.

• • •

He began to seek me out after this, talking to me whenever he got a chance. His face held a charge, like the electric air before a storm. The discontentment. I felt I was floating in space on a mobile, moving through air without a real home, and I recognized this charge: energy that wants to express itself in a transfer. Mostly, he talked about painting. At first I tolerated him, but as time went on my interest grew. He spoke with such authority and passion about painting theory and history and technique, the vocabulary of the brushstroke, I began to wish I could believe in a miracle. Maybe he could paint without the benefit of decent sight, what with the force of five decades of practice? Those decades must have value. But then he could make out only the brightest colors and sharpest forms. He told me so. I had a hard time believing even the most practiced hand could overcome this, except in dreams.

What is a life? I wondered. A practice? Can it continue to move through space once it dies? The people who had died recently and who I thought of often in those days felt more fully alive to me than they had in life.

One of them, a close friend, had killed four people. The accident sent his car up in flames after the engine exploded, and I had watched it burn by the side of the highway in a photograph online before his body was identified, when the police were calling around to see if he was alive.

My first thought that day: I need to call him.

But of course at that point, at that temperature, there was no longer a cell phone to call.

I sat alone in my studio in Virginia now, and I thought of calling him.

He would pick up and say, "Hello?"

And I would say, "Oh, thank god."

"Why?" he would ask, surprised, and I would tell him what I was seeing.

We would discuss how his car had been stolen, the misunderstanding. His car, in which he drove me home on that same stretch of road one July afternoon.

It was hard to say his name.

In my novel, people moved around rooms. They picked up objects, spoke to each other. I couldn't find it in myself to care. I changed their genders, but that did not help. It did, however, make the novel more unexpected. Perhaps the old painter's work would be the same way: heedless, surprising. But that was, of course, no substitute for vision.

Aaron, whose studio was across from mine, was making a monumental abstract drawing. Or painting, rather: he sketched lines in pencil and went over them with brown ink. He made the ink by boiling black walnuts for hours in an old tin pot on the stove. He would invite me to sit and talk with him as he worked. I liked to lean against the wall, watching as he moved around the studio, washing brushes and sharpening pencils and putting on music and finding snacks for us. A week into my stay, I was sitting in his studio with him and a new resident, a microtonal composer with a special love for making scatological jokes, and I decided to ask them if they knew why the old painter used the surgical tape on his face. The men both shrugged. The question did not seem to interest them. Have you seen his paintings yet? I asked, and they shook their heads no. To his knowledge, Aaron said, no one had been invited to visit the old painter's studio. This was not unusual. The idea was we should have total privacy if we so desired, privacy I often used to take a nap.

"Do you think they're any good?" I asked Aaron. The microtonal composer and I sat watching Aaron trace lines on his enormous painting, which was coming to resemble a vector.

"They can't be," Aaron said.

The microtonal composer made a farting noise.

Aaron and I looked at him, startled.

"That's *my* best guess," he said.

"You two aren't very nice."

"But you know we're right," the composer replied.

Sophie walked by, humming to herself.

"Join us," Aaron called to her. He had a crush on her; many of the men did. She was striking, with high cheekbones and cheeks perpetually flushed a sweet pink. She was friendly but disappeared a lot and was therefore mysterious. She'd shown me a picture of the boyfriend in South Africa, whom she'd met while volunteering at an orphanage. He was tall and handsome, with the straight white teeth of an underwear model. His parents were wealthy, and he wanted her to come live with him on their family estate outside Johannesburg, but she had her doubts. Go live with him! I'd urged. What do you have to lose?

She wandered in.

Our conversation veered away from the old painter. Aaron looked at Sophie with such intense but expertly veiled longing that I began to hope she would break up with her South African and leave him to save orphans on his own. She liked Aaron, it was clear. But Aaron did not strike me as the kind of guy who would ultimately settle down with a girl like Sophie, nor she a person who would ultimately be happy with a guy as gently goofy as Aaron, so I continued to hope for her sake she would go to South Africa and have lots of great sex with the rich boy who loved her. If it seemed too good to be true, well, enjoy it while you could. Life was increasingly like this: full of impossible, contradictory wishes.

What can I tell you about my life at that time? It was a quiet life, constrained. I spoke little. I smiled. My friends did not know my true desires, my longings. I lived in a hot place far from home. The man I was engaged to marry was patient, the sort of person who never spoke over you in conversation. He waited to be sure you were done talking, and he waited a few extra seconds beyond. When I told him that my friend had died, he waited. He did not rush to console me. This might be why I had said yes when he asked me to marry him, a word I had never been able to say to another person. And when I said I was going here, to Virginia, he did not complain, said only, "Do good work."

On the telephone, I lied to him. I said the novel was coming along. I said the fresh air and sunshine were inspiring. I said—but this was true, or mostly true—that I missed him. I entertained him with stories about

Aaron and Sophie and their thwarted love affair. I did not mention the old painter. I suppose I was waiting until I had more to report, though what that more might be, I did not yet know.

I kept hoping the old painter would invite me to visit his studio. He didn't, though I dropped hints, and once, in violation of the rules, he stood outside my studio wondering loudly if anyone had seen me until I emerged. "Did you need something?" I asked him, irritated, although of course I had been doing nothing aside from staring at a blank sheet of paper—or rather a backlit replica of a blank sheet of paper—and he said he had merely wanted to know what time I was going to eat lunch.

Tuesday at breakfast a few days later, the invitation came at last. The old painter asked me to visit his studio that afternoon, but only if I was interested, of course, he added anxiously, saying he would understand if I was otherwise occupied. I promised I was not. Well then, he said, come by between two p.m. and four p.m. He worked best when the light was strongest, so I was to drop in after that part of the day was over. I spent the next hours in my studio waiting impatiently for two o'clock to come, feeling, crazily, I knew, but nonetheless urgently, that in seeing his work I would learn something important.

"Come in," he called at my tap, and, when I opened the door, "Thank you for coming."

The place was airy, bright: large windows on three sides, a bed in the corner. On the radio, classical music, a light sound with strings and a piano. The back door, propped open, allowed in March sunlight and a hard, cold breeze.

He shut the door to the hallway, his cane clattering on the handle. Lingering by the door, as if reluctant to allow me in any farther, he told me he was thinking of departing the day after tomorrow, five days early.

"If I leave with Henry I must begin to pack. He's offered to drive me to New York. But I don't know whether I should leave."

"Do you feel you've finished your work here?" I asked him.

"No, but I've been anxious. Unsettled."

"About missing New York? Wanting to be home?"

"No. Not that. Maybe about returning."

"How would you go?"

"The train."

"I like the train, looking out the windows at the landscape."

"I don't like it. I dread it a little."

"Did you always dislike it?"

"No, since my vision has gone. It's harder, all of it. A ride from door to door would be a relief. But if I go with him, I need to start packing today."

Beyond where we stood, two white folding tables made a T. On these tables his paintings were arranged in long rows, two deep. We moved toward them. "They're all vertical," he said. "Arranged in the order I finished them. Which would you like to see first?"

The perhaps forty paintings were done on rectangular sheets of paper about fifteen inches by twelve inches. They were color field paintings made with acrylic and pastel so the paper's grain was visible at the edges. The initial paintings were dark. They looked overworked. The middle paintings were best: unmuddied, quick and loose. One juxtaposed a deep blue with a bright orange. Another was green and white. The later paintings were simple, plain and undone.

"You choose," I said.

He lifted a painting from the nearest table. A violet mass in the center, yellow at the sides. "Some of these I work and work. This one came quickly." He selected a murky painting, red laid over black, four raised circles in the center arrayed like bushes rising up from the paper. "I work with a very wet brush. This makes me think of fire, and of trees. But I shouldn't say that. I don't like to influence the viewer." Next, a dove gray painting from the back table, a royal blue streak on the left side, a loose black textural stripe forming a small curve reminiscent of a heart. "This one is for my friend who is a poet. She helped me with these immensely. It's an elegant painting."

He held a brownish yellow painting close to his face, perhaps a foot away. "How well can you see it?" I asked. We stood near the open door, sunlight on the paper. In the light the solid color field disintegrated, lighter streaks showing. "I did this one with the walnut ink that man made. What is his name?" "Aaron." "Yes, him. It's a beautiful, rich color."

It was not. Aaron had boiled and boiled the walnuts in a pot on the stove to leech the color, but he had grown frustrated. He'd gathered more walnuts from the grounds. Still the color was not deep. But he used it nonetheless: it was cheaper than buying ink. A failure, he'd said, but not a total failure. It was important to work quickly, he believed, so you could blow through your mistakes.

"Here I can begin to see detail," he said, "the texture of the strokes and the paper." He moved the painting around, a few inches from his face, scrutinizing small parts. "But it's blurry."

I described the lighter places, gesturing to where the field became a pale amber. "I'm glad to know that," he said. "But in artificial light, in a museum or gallery, you might not see it. The lighting in galleries is always so bad."

He chose the most recent painting on the table, last in its row, done in a wash of dark green. "What feeling does this give you?"

I thought about it. The word I thought was melancholy, but that seemed too gentle. "Dark," I said. "A dark feeling."

"Yes," he said. "I was feeling very down. I ran out of energy."

"Despondent," I said.

"Yes," he said. "Despondent."

"If I leave with Henry, I should begin packing today. But I don't know."

"It would be a shame to leave when you're feeling that way," I said. "Maybe you should stay."

"There's no guarantee it would change," he said. "But it is beautiful here, and New York is so ugly."

"In March?"

"All the time."

He touched my arm. "When are you getting married?"

"October, I think."

"He's very lucky."

I thanked him for showing me his paintings, said goodbye, and slipped out. Closing the door, the cane rattled on the door handle. I heard a pause, and then him taking up the cane and moving slowly toward the stereo, turning it up, the sound of the classical music swelling.

So I had my answer. The paintings were, for the most part, childlike. The compositions had a minimalist appeal, but his execution was sometimes sloppy, the paper cheap—likely all he could afford, given the volume he produced—and any moments of grace accidental. What's more, they were like Rothko's work, but decades too late. He was like an athlete who could no longer compete but kept training. But at dinner that night, he said he was energized by our visit and no longer thinking of leaving early; he would perhaps even host an open studio. "Other people have asked about my work," he told me, "and after your visit, I'm encouraged."

I felt obscurely guilty; although I hadn't lied to him, I also hadn't told him the truth. At the same time, this was the happiest I'd seen him, and surely that was no small thing. He said that when I'd left his studio, he'd thought he was done for the day but had instead begun working again, new paintings coming easily.

Around us, others discussed New York. Talk turned to the storm. He joined the conversation. He had lost power for a week after Sandy. An explosion at the Con Edison power station had knocked out electricity in Lower Manhattan. He announced to the table: "After the storm it was remarkable. It was like there were two New Yorks: above Fortieth Street and below Fortieth Street. Damp and cold and no heat, and the people above Fortieth Street were living their lives as if nothing had happened."

"On the contrary," the Dutch sculptor named Ilse corrected him, for she, too, lived in New York, "I found that people were very kind and helpful. Not like in the seventies; no looting. In stores people handed you what you needed. 'Do you need this? Do you need this?' And they handed it to you."

"Well, I don't know about that."

"Do you have neighbors?" she asked. "Neighbors are important, David."

"How people could do nothing, I don't understand."

"Do you have neighbors?"

"I do. I have one neighbor, and he amazed me. He walked all over the city to get food. He must have walked twenty miles."

I asked about his life in the city. He had a closed-circuit television in his apartment, he said. He could put a book on the ledge and the television illuminated the page. The font could be made larger and darker and flipped from black on white to white on black. He listened to stories broadcast from Symphony Space, but it wasn't the same as a book: you couldn't go back and reread if your mind wandered. Each word was briefly there and gone. An old art teacher of his had taken him to hear Dylan Thomas read at the Kaufmann Auditorium in 1950, when he was in high school. Her husband was a poet, no longer well known, but included in the Weinberger anthology of American poetry. She loved Thomas. So did her husband. Thomas read "A Child's Christmas in Wales" and "Do Not Go Gentle." Norma Millay was a friend; she had recited her sister Edna St. Vincent's poems from memory, quite a cut-up, and done voices like Tallulah Bankhead. He laughed a little at this memory. "You know Tallulah Bankhead?" he asked me. "The story about the little brown monkey she carried onto the stage during *Conchita* who snatched the wig from her head and ran off, and she turned a cartwheel and the whole audience applauded? She writes of it in her autobiography."

"Another story goes," he went on, "that a friend of hers brought a fresh young man to a party, a bit of a wit, and he told her he was taken by her—she was beautiful—and that he wanted to make love to her that evening, and she replied, 'And so you shall, you wonderful, old-fashioned boy.'"

· · ·

After this he was happier, more sociable; at the same time, his dependence upon me grew. The next night at dinner, as I was busy talking to Aaron, the old German woman with the cap of black hair leaned in and began to speak to the painter urgently and quickly in her sparrow voice, sonorous and accented and hard to discern. She waited always for him, around corners, at the table, seeking him out, and once had stood by herself in a room, her hands clenched into fists, muttering about how he ignored her and liked to speak only to the younger women.

He stopped smiling and turned away. When I spoke to him, he said nothing, as though to punish me.

But later that evening, he joined a group to watch television. Five of us were watching *Girls* in the living room, near the staircase. From the top of the stairs, he overheard dialogue. He shouted, "I hear dirty talk! I'm coming down." We sat on the couch, huddled together drinking red wine, so he pulled up a chair behind the couch and listened; he couldn't see anyway. He kept mishearing, pestering us to repeat what the characters had said. Finally, I turned around and repeated, "He said, 'I'm going to eat your pussy on the sidewalk.'"

"Aren't you glad you asked, David?" Ilse scolded him, as he sat in shock, and we all laughed. He laughed too.

At the end of the episode, he asked me, puzzled, "This was written by a woman?"

"Yes," I said.

"And this show is considered feminist?"

"It is," I said.

"Times change, I guess," he said.

My chest began to unclench, and I thought briefly I was about to start writing again. But Saturday, bombs exploded in Boston. I had lived there after college, and the street was familiar to me, a place I often walked. The hours took on a strange, insulated quality. I read everything I could. Footage was eerily distant and close at the same time. Our wireless connection did not work in our studios, so I took out my cell phone in my dorm room and hit refresh, hunched over its face like it was a set of tarot cards. I had a sense the news might change. But of course all the phone's screen could tell me was what was past.

On a walk before breakfast on Sunday, I came across a deer skeleton, flesh worn away by rain and air. The ribcage was beautiful. It was a poem. But even if the violence of death was a poem, it was still death.

At breakfast Aaron invited me to go to church with him and Sophie. The church was a historic black Baptist church; the director had mentioned it, and they wanted to learn about the history. I said yes. I did not believe and did not want to intrude, and I regretted my answer as soon as I spoke, but I didn't know how to say I'd changed my mind. Once the three of us arrived, though, I was happy to be in a space I could sit with my thoughts amidst other people.

To open the proceedings, the reverend led us in giving thanks for all that we had. "I woke up today and I had the use of my limbs. I had eyes that could see. Thank you, Lord, for legs that can walk. Thank you, Lord, for eyes that can see." Our voices followed his: "Thank you, Lord, for legs that can walk. Thank you, Lord, for eyes that can see."

Once we were done singing the hymn, the reverend began his sermon. "The men in Boston, they wanted to do what God does, to take life, Lord have mercy on us. Don't fail your test. Your children: you may have children, and they may be disobedient. Don't fail your test. Monday, you may go to work and a person may not look you in the eye, may not say, How you doing? Don't fail your test."

As he preached, he shuffled his feet and gave a soft "huh" to punctuate his words. The effect was electric. It made me feel the words inside.

He wore a long white robe. By the altar, peonies.

Descending the stairs, he paused, gazing out: "And you may find that, like Adam and Eve, the weakness of the flesh is upon *you*. Our brothers and sisters in the Senate, they failed their test. Those men in Boston, they failed their test. Don't fail *your* test."

At the altar now, he called to us: "There may be some here today who want to be saved. You may come forward now."

I wanted it, but I did not believe it was possible.

A woman in a gold-brimmed hat shifted in the pew ahead but did not rise. The right side of her face was speckled with many small, dark beauty marks. Paper fans had been distributed. They featured an advertisement for a funeral home, with a photograph of a serious man in a dark suit, red handkerchief in a breast pocket, and now she lifted her arm and fanned her face. The man's face moved as she fanned, replacing hers and revealing it, replacing and revealing.

An old woman wearing a purple suit slowly rose and made her way to the altar.

"Don't fail your test," the preacher implored as she walked, looking out at us. His eyes were light, luminous yellow feldspar set in a field of white sclera.

Before dinner on Monday, I walked in defeat to the main residence. It had been a long, quiet day alone in my studio without a thing to say. At dinner, the London printmaker who so disliked the old painter announced that she was having an open studio the following afternoon. He was displeased and muttered to me about it; he claimed he had been thinking of having his open studio tomorrow. Of course, he had said nothing about it, so he had no right to be upset. He retired early.

I wasn't especially interested in the printmaker's work, but unable to stand the solitude of my studio the next afternoon, I decided to drop by. I went alone and stood with the others around the printmaker in an attentive semicircle. She rolled an orange soy-based ink onto a clear plastic plate with a small roller, the sticky ink spreading slowly. The paper she had initially been using, she explained, had been the wrong type, Stonehenge paper, and so the ink would not dry, because it did not dry, really; instead, the ink was absorbed into the paper. Before a show she had tried drying her prints with a hairdryer and heating them over the radiator, but the ink never set. Now she used a new kind of paper. This paper she soaked in water and lay between sheets of plastic to keep wet.

On the walls the printmaker had hung small prints reminiscent of wallpaper. She liked to use a grid pattern and a dot pattern.

Two women leaned in, examining a twelve-inch lavender medallion print, wineglasses in hand. Other people talked in small clusters. The old painter entered, stood alone. He had been very peevish since she had announced the open studio, and I did not join him; I felt worn down. I was not sure if he could see I was there. I doubted it.

The printmaker put the orange-inked plate on her drafting table and lifted a piece of damp white paper from the stack. "I've heard heavier paper is best," she said. "Back in London, I'm going to try it."

"Have you tried watercolor paper?" he asked.

"No," she said. She spoke matter-of-factly. "It's textured. Well, some of it isn't, I suppose, but this paper works."

"Oh," he said.

The printing press was electric-powered. She registered the damp paper with a cardboard edge, aligning it, lifted the edge, and fed the paper into the metal roller. The roller needed to grip the edge of the paper before she laid down the plate.

He picked up a bottle of Akua ink and held it close to his face.

"Is the ink made in Japan?" he asked.

"America," she said. "A North Carolina–based operation recently bought the company."

She put down the inked plate and ran the press. She wiped traces of ink from the press's Plexiglas surface and laid down a second plate. "Middle-aged eyes," she said, setting her glasses on the press.

"Better not forget to pick your glasses up," the old painter said.

She did not respond.

He moved nearer, leaning on his cane.

She ran the press again, using the orange print as the base, and held up the result. Dribs and drabs of gold paint had made blotches over the orange. We gathered around. She showed us the print, rotating slowly inside the circle of people.

The old painter pressed forward, putting his face near the paper so he could see.

"Okay, David," she said brusquely, moving it away from him to prevent him from accidentally brushing against it, "I'm going to put this on the table to dry, and you can look at it over there."

People began to talk. The old painter followed her to the table and examined the print. He had to lean down to get his face close enough to the paper to see, but he did not lift the paper himself. Instead, he stooped. His hands were clasped behind his back. He appeared to want to demonstrate that he would not touch it. He stayed that way for two minutes or so, hunched over the print. Then, without speaking to anyone, he stood upright and made his slow way to the door.

Outside, April was in bloom. Through the shared bathroom I heard noises from Sophie's room that could only mean one thing: Aaron was getting his wish, and her South African boyfriend had reason to fear for her loyalty. Of course, they said nothing to me. Still, I was happy for them. Mornings, I sat on a stone bench beneath one especially enormous horse chestnut tree as chilly sunlight filtered down. The pale pink blossoms emitted an acerbic scent, like diluted bleach. My characters talked amongst themselves. I strained to hear them, but they wanted privacy. They were being mysterious; they moved away from me. I wondered who they were. Were they people I remembered? Were they the dead, come back? Or were they only me, myself, an echo?

Those days spent collecting data, recording the results: I had thought that writing would be the same. But in the end, it wasn't; it required more.

I had nothing to say. I could hear nothing. I decided to quit. It was the honorable thing to do.

The painter was upset by the open studio visit. He wouldn't say so, but his feelings were deeply hurt and he held a grudge. His mood plunged. In response he decided to hold his own open studio in two days, to compete with the London woman. He would be more popular: I think that was his hope. He hung up signs on doors with the date and time written in a large, shaky hand and positioned right at eye level. Then he began to worry that no one would come. At breakfast he pestered people, wanting them to insist on visiting. He would ask if they had seen his sign, saying he was concerned the sign was easy to miss if a person was not paying attention. Then he would say he hoped he would not be overrun with visitors, as he tired easily. But of course he hoped they knew he didn't mean *them*, he would add; he would certainly want *them* to come, if they felt the event was of interest.

He carried a small white box with a clock and a mechanical voice. A tone would sound and the soft female voice would announce the time. As he encouraged people to come to his open studio, the voice would interject: Eight a.m. Eight fifteen a.m. Eight thirty a.m. Eight forty-five a.m. Nine a.m.

At night now, he preferred to retreat to his room and play classical music on his small stereo. He would tap his way up with his cane and leave the door ajar. He didn't take care of himself as well as he might. He gave off the warm, human smell of flesh lived in. It was not entirely unpleasant. It was the smell of an older person who did not like to wash more than was necessary. The smell grew stronger, became that of a person turned a little feral.

In my studio, I read. I was done writing.

I was afraid, but I fed the horse outside my studio window an apple left from lunch, holding it out to him open palmed, as I had been taught as a girl. His teeth were big and yellowed, nostrils large, and when he moved away my hand was wet.

"I'm coming home to you," I said on the telephone, and while the love of another person was not enough to make up for what I could not do, it was what I had now, and I was grateful the way a person was grateful now to have legs.

The day of the open studio came. I tried to enlist Sophie and Aaron to go with me; the old painter was so nervous and I wanted to make him happy. The three of us arriving at once might do it: he would feel admired, loved. We weren't exactly a crowd, which is what he kept worrying over and obviously wanting, but we were a respectable group. Sophie said she was busy. Aaron was curious and said yes.

"Let's go early," I said, "to encourage him."

"We'd better," Aaron agreed, "or he might cancel the whole thing."

The painter had been in a dark mood at breakfast, convinced no one would stop by. But people had; we'd already seen a few returning, including the old German woman who held a torch for him, and when Aaron and I arrived, he was happy. "Come in, come in!" he said, opening the door. "I heard you giggling down the hall."

It was noon; he was not going to paint today because he left the next day and was worried the new work would not dry. The back door was open, but the studio was not so cold this time. The morning chill had abated, the April wind less punishing than the cold March gusts.

"You came before the crowds. If there will be crowds this afternoon—I don't know."

He had done a new painting the day of my visit, a true pink with a streak of white on the right side. "You see," he said to me, "after we spoke my mood changed." He picked it up from the table carefully, holding it by its edges, and carried it to the open door where the natural light was strong. Holding it to the light, his brown hand with its flat nails trembled.

The new painting came alive in the sunlight. It was pleasing, cheerful and tranquil.

Aaron asked if next we could see the graphic blue-and-gray painting, which he had spotted on the table. The painter slowly made his way back to the table to fetch it and brought it to the doorway. With its higher contrast of values, in the bright daylight, it became more subtle.

"It was very calm," he said, "the blue and the gray, and I decided it needed punch. I picked up a black pastel and zip! it had punch. But it's a total risk enterprise. I could as easily have—zip!—spoiled it."

Aaron went back to the tables to fetch the yellowish walnut ink painting, hoping, I suppose, to spare the painter the trip, though the painter followed close behind him, and he dropped it in a clumsy movement. The painting fell facedown on another painting. Aaron flinched as it fell. "I'm so sorry," he said quickly, reaching for it and holding it gently. "But these aren't wet. Thank god they aren't wet anymore."

"They aren't, no," the painter said. He was displeased. He grabbed the painting from Aaron and hobbled to the door. Examining it closely in the light, he seemed to settle down, to find the strength to hide his irritation.

"From now on, let me do the handling," he said.

Aaron bowed his head in apology, and then, realizing the old painter couldn't see this gesture, said apologetically, "Yes, that's best."

The painter took up a blue painting. A velvety density of color gathered at the left, where the acrylic was thickest, and the middle faded to a lighter blue. On the right, a pearly pastel took over. Light blue washes like a thin watercolor stippled this portion, and in the sunlight, a faint pink iridescence rose up.

"The dots are like a consolation," Aaron said.

"Which dots?" the painter asked.

"Here, in the light, almost like glitter from beneath."

"I can't see that. It's mysterious to me, what these paintings do."

The two men stood in the sun. "How did you get this color?" Aaron asked.

"I worked acrylic into pastel, both wet. I don't know exactly. I add, and the paintings change. This one was mostly purple at first."

"It's amazing how you hide the brushstrokes."

"In the center the surface is so smooth," I said, "and then the rough edge."

"In the seventies," the old painter said, "there was a bar on the Lower East Side where the artists hung out. We would talk about painting. This was when hard lines were what people were doing; they'd use masking tape to get those hard edges. And what people would ask would be, 'Are you hard-edge or soft-edge?' It used to be, 'Are you figural or abstract?' So this was the new question. And my friend came up with a good answer." He laid down the painting. "He would say," and here he put his hands in the air and waved them maniacally, "'I'm *on* edge!'"

"I've always been about showing the process. An art critic from the nineteenth century said that there were two kinds of painters: sun painters and moon painters. The sun painters showed the process. The moon painters erased it. Vermeer was a moon painter."

He set the blue painting on an empty easel by the door. We all examined it without speaking.

"Matisse would erase what he'd done each day. He'd paint all day and at the end of the day wipe the paint away so there was only a ghost image, and the next day he'd begin again. He has a painting called *Pink Nude*, a pink figure reclining. These lines behind." He drew a grid in the air with his hand. "He worked on that painting for seven or eight months, and it looks like it was painted in an afternoon. *New York* magazine did a spread on it, showing the evolution of the painting."

"Another moon painter," I said.

"Yes."

"He'd have his assistant wipe the paintings, I heard," Aaron said. "What a strange job, wiping away his work."

The painter ignored him and addressed me: "The article talks about his sybaritic side, and it's true: Matisse loved pleasure. His work has a deceptive ease. When you said the work shows in one painting of mine, that was an astute comment: the work should not show."

"It's hard to do," I said.

"'Profound and lucid sight,' the critic says. That was the *Pink Nude*."

"Will you change this one now?" I asked.

"One painter I knew, he'd go in and rework his old paintings. He didn't have very many, and he kept reworking them. He couldn't ever stop. For me, once it's finished, good or bad, it's done. I don't go back in and change it."

We all fell silent, our eyes on the small blue painting, whose pink iridescence withdrew itself from us as the sun dimmed behind a cloud.

"I'll begin packing this afternoon," the painter said to me. "I leave tomorrow on the train."

"I'm happy to help," Aaron said.

"Thank you," the painter said. "I might need assistance carrying my valise back to the residence."

He was growing tired. We thanked him for inviting us, and he thanked us for coming and walked us to the door. "You beat the crowds," he said, "although I don't know if there will be crowds."

On my way out, I asked him, "What is that word? I couldn't think of it. The word for *overwork*."

"Oh," he said, happy, "*iberpotshke*. Why? You want to use it?"

"Perhaps."

Aaron had gone ahead. I turned to go, and the painter reached out to delay me. "Remember, my dear," he said gently, "for the abstract expressionists, there were two things: action and hesitation. And only one was worth something."

As the painter waited in the residence lobby for a cab to the train, I came down to say goodbye. By his feet sat his battered brown suitcase. He held a black portfolio bag containing all the paintings he had done. He was taking them with him back to the city. I asked how he would store them. "Well, I have flat storage, and so on, archival boxes."

He took from his bag a final painting he had made, a light gray painting. "There are a million different grays. Complementary colors make a gray: violet and yellow, for example."

The painting had a muted, haunting quality. It reminded me of mist rising off the winter ocean. It was by far my favorite. I admired the subtle mottling and striations. Whether or not he knew it, they were beautiful. I told him so. He brought the painting up to his face. "Gee, I wish I could see that."

I thought he might intend to give me this gray painting, but he took the painting back. His gesture was protective, a bit triumphant. He tucked it in his valise.

"What will you do when you get home?" I asked.

"I don't know. I wish I could take the landscape and the air and the silence."

"What is it like where you live?" he asked after a pause. "Is it turbulent where the two oceans meet or do they get along?"

"It's hot," I said, honestly. "Hot and strange."

"Will you write to me?" he asked. "If I give you my address?"

"Of course," I said, though we both knew I wouldn't.

He departed for his train, paintings in tow. I watched him make his way to the cab. He did not want help out, though I offered. "Write me," he said again. I never did, and he never wrote me, either. But after he left I went to my room and looked up the article he had quoted, the one that praised Matisse's profound and lucid sight. I read it often, and, when at last I began to write again, I pinned it over my desk. It was by Kay Larson. He had gotten the quote right. She herself was quoting a curator's assessment. Of Matisse's life, she writes: "At times he surges forward with a new idea, as the confusion of influences under which he has been laboring suddenly sorts itself out. At other times, he draws back and gathers his energy, a process that can take years or even decades. Sometimes, both states exist in the same moment, linked by the courage to dare even to fail." "If you're like me," she adds, "this show will bring you to your knees."

Seeing Clear

MY FATHER'S SUICIDE attempts began when I was ten. He worked at killing himself more earnestly than he had any job. First, it wasn't overt, just lots and lots of cocaine. Then, when that failed to do anything other than get him high and in debt to the sorts of people you'd rather not be in debt to, he switched approaches. A string of overdoses followed, along with a pretty severe beating. Next came the botched murder-suicide that left my mother with bruises on her neck and him asleep in a motel room for four days. The constitution of an ox, the police said. That many pills would've killed anyone else.

After that, he was put on a plane to a rehab facility in Florida. The bill was paid not by us, because we were broke, but by his mother, who had a little money with which to intervene in the disaster he was quickly making of all our lives by, you know, threatening to end them. He wasn't a quitter, though, so out of rehab, he set about the business again. His binges left me stranded after school until he came to and remembered me. Agnes and I would hang around the Putney Central payphone in the echoey gymnasium, watching the seventh-grade boys shoot hoops and lying when a teacher passing by asked if we needed a ride home. If he didn't show by five, when the janitor locked up the school, we'd walk the two miles to our mother's house and skip that week's visit.

Finally, he decided to go for a more surefire method, one that had worked for his brother years before. He drove into a tree going seventy-five miles an hour, no seatbelt. Flew straight out the windshield and broke his neck. I don't know how he was discovered, but he was, bloody and lying in the road. A helicopter airlifted him to Mary Hitchcock, where I guess it was touch and go for a while. In any case, he survived. At first they thought he'd be paralyzed, but even that fear proved unfounded. I didn't visit him in the hospital. I wanted him to die, was sick of the waiting. Sick of sitting on the edge of his bed in his dingy apartment with empty walls while he lay comatose, staring at the black-and-white television that only got one station. Not that it mattered—he stared at the TV even when it was off. But he lived. "Just like the goddamned Energizer Bunny," in my mother's words. That was the end of the suicide attempts. Why, I don't know, because that was also the end of our weekly visits, but his lawyer claimed he'd found God. He did seem better, even in the depressing atmosphere of family court, but I doubted this explanation. More likely, it had to do with the lithium he was prescribed and the twenty-two-year-old he met in AA, a dreamy girl with the vacant eyes of a person who'd done acid one too many times and who came with him to court in a blazer and lipstick, looking like she wanted to be an adult.

Though his attempts failed, suicide was always there, staring at me from above like a malevolent guardian angel. In high school, I began to consider the possibility. Even through my misery, I didn't think I'd do it, but knowing it was an option helped me get through the days. By my senior year, when I was fifteen, I thought about it less and about the possibility of attending college more, imagining it to be a sort of utopia full of books and interesting people and leafy paths, a place I might walk straight out of my unhappiness and into a brochure. I'd pretty much stopped thinking about my father too, until one late January afternoon—evening, really; dusk had fallen—when my mother came into my bedroom, where I sat reading my physics textbook. "Net force experienced by an object," it said, "is determined by computing the vector sum of all individual forces acting upon that object." My mother stood in the doorway, surveyed the mess, and sighed.

"What are you working on?" she asked.

I read her the theorum.

"Well," she said, "I'd like to see the formula that can account for all that." Then she looked at me in silence until I said, "Mom?"

She had spoken with his new girlfriend, Skye, on the phone. They'd been together off and on for a year; she was a decade younger and divorced. My father had stopped returning Skye's calls, my mother said, and she had grown alarmed. When she let herself into his apartment, his place looked normal. A bender? she wondered. But she asked around and none of his friends had seen him. Finally, she called his employer. It turned out he hadn't shown up at the timber lot for five days. So Skye called the police, who my mother doubted were looking too hard for him.

"Leave it to your father to pull a stunt like this," she said. "Maybe he's decided to do us all a favor and disappear for good."

"Maybe," I said.

I didn't think about his disappearance much that week. It wasn't like his absence was anything new. He was already an absence, an address on the labels of the magazines he subscribed to as a birthday present for me and sent over through his lawyer. One package had come with a note saying that he wanted to make amends. He had spelled it with two *m*s, and this, more than anything, had made me sad. Briefly, I'd considered calling him. Then I forced myself to think about all the times he had chosen other things over my safety, the times he'd talked about taking me to Mexico or Canada, where my mother couldn't find me, because I was his favorite child, I was the one who understood him, and I hadn't picked up the phone. Now, I just sort of assumed they'd find him unconscious in another hotel room, he'd get shipped to another rehab center, and the custody battles would come to a temporary standstill. Or that he'd be found dead, and the custody battles would cease.

But my mother's words proved prophetic; my father hadn't quit on us yet. He resurfaced several weeks later in the form of a postcard addressed to me, which I collected from the mailbox that capped our icy drive. On the front was a photograph of the desert. The back was blank, except for where he'd written my name and address:

Kate Bishop
7 Orchard Hill Road
Putney, VT 05346

There was no return address, but the postmark was from Arizona. Belen, the blurred-out stamp read.

The winter's freshness had worn off, and the pine trees' needles were sparse, the crusted snow at the driveway's edges caked and dirty. It was freezing, but I stood outside by the mailbox holding the postcard until my fingers went numb and the inside of my nose was so stung with cold it stopped running. I tried to imagine the Southwest. All I could think of was flatness and desert. I couldn't see my born-and-bred-in-New England father in a desert. I looked at his handwriting, spare, almost severe, then turned the postcard over and contemplated the landscape. It looked innocuous enough, just whitish sand and cactus and highway. I knew that I should give the postcard to the police, but I decided to keep it. I didn't know what good it would do anyone to know my father might be in Arizona. I'd probably just have to fill out some sort of form and they'd call the postcard evidence and take it, and it would sit in a drawer somewhere, collecting dust.

Putting first one hand in my jacket pocket to warm it and then the other, I studied the picture. The sand shimmered, the cactus was greenly opaque, and the highway, which bisected the sand in a sharp, straight diagonal, was nondescript, just black pavement held down by two yellow lines. It led to the horizon, where the clear blue of the sky hit the sand so hard it seemed like there should be a black line separating the two. The sand and sky and highway and cactus were frustratingly blank. I couldn't read anything in them. I turned the postcard over and looked at the white where a message should be. Only the handwritten address gave the sender away. I folded the postcard in half and stuck it in my pocket.

Several weeks later, the second postcard arrived. I'd carried the first one every day, and the edges had been battered soft. The fold was pronounced from the many times I'd pulled it out and looked at it, each time unfolding and refolding it. In comparison, the second postcard looked pristine. It too had a desertscape on the front. It was postmarked Ash Fork, New Mexico, and again offered just my name and address, no more. The desert in this picture was very much like the last one, only there was no road, just sand and sky, and it was nighttime. The clarity of the light was remarkable. Because of the flatness, the land wasn't the tangle of shadows I was used to. Instead, there were planes, paper-flat and shining. Again, I failed to see through the image into what it was my father wanted me to understand.

Spring came, wet and chilly. Along our road pussy willows budded, soft silvery-gray nubs spotting the low branches. Yellow forsythia blossoms opened on the bushes near our house and muddy ruts slicked the road. I kept waiting for another postcard to appear in the mailbox and was careful to collect the mail before my mother did, but weeks went by and none arrived. Graduation, on the other hand, approached rapidly. I found myself getting angrier and angrier. Other fathers gave their children tuition money or secondhand Volkswagens or at least some decent advice, something practical or meaningful to use as they left home. All my father had given me were two postcards with nothing on the back.

It was around that time that the hang-up calls started. My mother figured it was the doing of teenage boys, bored prank callers. If she picked up and no one responded, she'd sigh, launch into a lecture—"Stop calling this number. You're wasting my time and your own"—until the other person ended the call. Usually, though, I was the one who answered the phone. I would just say, "Hello? Is someone there?" and then wait quietly until the caller hung up. The silence on the other end was never broken except once, when the operator's voice intervened asking for more change. Every time, I strained to hear something, but always failed. I couldn't ever hang up first, though. I don't know why, but I couldn't make myself. Maybe it felt too defensive, or maybe I was just used to waiting.

The day after graduation, one more postcard came. Again, a photograph of the desert with just my address and a stamp on the back. The postmark had bled, and I couldn't read the town—it looked like it began with an *S*, or maybe an *E*—but the state abbreviation was Nevada's. In this one, the road had reappeared, but the cactus was gone. Just road and sand and sky were caught by the sunrise, splashed red and orange.

That night, the phone rang, and I answered it to hear the same silence on the other end. I waited, and then asked hesitantly, "Dad?"

After a minute, my father's voice came through the line, scratchy and faint, but as unmistakable to me as his handwriting. "When I was there," he said, "I could see where I was, but that was all. Just where I was. Out here, I can finally see clear to where I'm going." There was a pause. A crackling noise rose and fell like the ocean, and then, before I could say anything, the phone went dead.

When people say they've found God, I'm always suspicious; my tendency is to think it's a case of mistaken identity. What they've found is their own mortality or guilt or the appeal of the idea of infinite love. Their certainty seems so presumptuous. The phrase is all wrong, too. God isn't a lost child, crying in the parking lot; if God did exist, wouldn't you *recognize* God rather than *find* God? So I wouldn't say my father found God at last out there in the desert. Maybe it was alcohol talking, some chemical imbalance, maybe he went off his lithium and thought he saw meaning where there was none. There's no way to know. The truth recedes faster than you can track it. What I believe, though, is that even if it was temporary, even if it wasn't something he could hang onto, he did find something. Not God, exactly; something realer, something here on earth—a solace of sorts, a lessening.

He died a few years later. It was an overdose. We got a call from a police station in California, and that was it. I looked at those postcards when I felt so lonely nothing could touch me, and I allowed myself to feel that lessening, however provisional, to move into that wide-open space. He wanted to leave me with that, at least, with this metaphor for what he felt but couldn't say. I suspect it was everything he had. In the end, maybe that's all any inheritance ever amounts to. And in the end, maybe it's never enough.

The Most Common State of Matter

OVER LUNCH, Kate's beautiful friend Josephine, with whom she taught at Louisiana State University, revealed that she was facing a health scare and needed Kate to drive her to a doctor's appointment for a procedure during which she would be put under twilight sedation. The fear was colon cancer, unlikely but grim. Jo was thirty-three, two years older than Kate, but Kate thought of them both as young, too young for tests. Girls, really. They were writers-in-residence, shared a cramped office. Jo was a poet. She wore brown leather cowboy boots with rosy-hued cotton skirts, and was debating whether to get bangs. The engine of her car, an ancient gray Volvo with a broken side mirror, was pretty much shot. The mechanics at the garage fixed it out of pity for her; they lost money on the repairs. Her life ran on charm.

They sat eating lunch at their desks, the door cracked open for air. Outside, the March sky was the color of pencil lead. Jo spread her apple slices and spinach salad before her and began picking at them without any real interest. Kate removed her tuna fish sandwich, to which she'd added sriracha for excitement. The hot sauce had bled through the bread. She liked the effect: batik.

"The doctor said he's going to look down my throat," Jo said, "and then flip me over."

Kate's mouth was full of tuna fish, but she raised her eyebrows and widened her eyes to suggest she found this disturbing.

"Those were his exact words," Jo continued. "'Flip me over.'"

"It sounds . . . unprofessional," said Kate.

"Doesn't it? It sounds bad."

"Date-rapey."

"I know. I wish he hadn't used that phrase."

"He didn't mean it that way, I'm sure."

"No. But still." Jo sighed. "You're under, and they can lift you up and move you like a rag doll. They can do whatever they want."

A plump-cheeked blonde girl of eighteen or so peeked into their office. Not recognizing either Kate or Jo, the girl drew back and said "Oops!" before walking away. This happened with surprising frequency. The students drifted across campus as if lost. They came into the wrong office and asked where Professor Mitchell was, or the psychology department, or whether they could borrow a stapler. Usually, Kate did not have an answer to their questions.

"Who *are* they?" Kate asked Jo. She and Jo both hailed from New England. They liked to discuss their confusion about the students.

"They run the gamut. What do you mean?"

"The crappy ones. The kinesiology majors."

"I assume they're all from Shreveport."

"Shreveport. Poor kids."

Jo smiled and twisted her hair up in a messy topknot. She was tall and slender. Her hair waved in a fetching way; this was the reason she had not gotten bangs. When she felt tension enter the room, she went blank, and her face took on a distant aspect. Had Kate and Jo been friends in high school, Kate knew, Jo would have been the girl at the party who left without telling anyone, the girl with the older boyfriend, the girl whose friendship was always in question because one was never sure she didn't have an entirely different set of cooler friends. They had met in August a year and a half ago after being assigned to share an office. Over her desk Jo had tacked a black-and-white photograph of Frank O'Hara, scowling down at them. Kate had liked it—and by extension Jo—before even meeting her. Jo seemed to understand Kate effortlessly. But then Jo's whole life looked effortless. This was not, of course, true; Kate knew better than to believe such a fantasy.

"Kate?" Eli called from the kitchen that evening.

She stood silent in the living room of their bungalow, holding a small leather box. Searching his coat pocket for the car keys, she had found this. She was quietly awed by her own panic. The unknown quality of its contours made her want to remain still and observe it. It had the vastness of a snowy field in winter, ringed with trees and glittering icily in the sunlight.

Should she open the box? She hesitated. She ran a finger over the lid. It felt like a once living thing, the leather supple and textured. Flipping the lid up, she found a platinum ring with a triangle of diamonds sparkling at its center.

They had never discussed engagement, at least not seriously.

"Kate?" his voice came again, more insistent.

Her heart jolted. She hadn't realized she was holding her breath until, at the sound of his voice, she exhaled. "One sec," she called.

She replaced the box and joined him in the pale-green-tiled kitchen, where he stood unpacking chicken breasts and tomatoes and Kalamata olives and the good salty feta cheese she liked. His gray suit jacket hung on a tall-backed stool by the kitchen island. He'd worn it to give a public presentation on the wetlands conservation work being done by the coastal sustainability studio he directed; he had shrugged the jacket off as soon as he walked in the door. He was happier out in the swamps and marshes, in jeans, collecting samples.

"Yes?" she asked.

Eli didn't answer right away. He put a small, lustrous cluster of variegated yellow heirloom tomatoes in the refrigerator, his lanky frame doubled to reach down low. He was tired from his presentation and irritated because after work she had been spaced out, vacant.

Rattled by Jo's disclosure, she had found herself unable to focus. "What was that?" she'd asked him in the car and failed to listen a second time, and he'd switched on the radio.

"Did you say you were going out?" he asked at last, turning from the refrigerator's thin light. He'd pushed up the sleeves of his white dress shirt, and the thick, soft hair on his arms shone gold.

"I did."

"Maybe you could pick up takeout."

"But you said you wanted to cook more."

"Yes, but I faced the public, and now I'm demoralized."

"I could make a salad," she offered.

"I need spicy food to burn away the memory."

"Fine," she said, softening.

"I'll call it in," he said. "Pad thai and green curry and that okra thing okay?"

"Whatever you want," she said. She smiled. He smiled back, all forgiven, and, moving past to place the call, put a friendly hand on her ass.

She drove to the takeout place. On her way, she stopped by Jo's apartment. The shades were drawn. Far back in the apartment a lamp glowed. Jo was, she bet, taking a bath. It was a habit she had when she was upset. Kate could use a quiet, soothing bath herself. The ring had discomfited her. She and Eli had been together three years, yes, but she still thought of the relationship as temporary. She liked things the way they were. Couldn't time just stop? She did not want to die. She did not want Jo to die. She did not want their lives to change. With the day's news, and now this development, things were moving in the wrong direction.

On Wednesday, in the waiting room before the test, Jo asked Kate to distract her. "Tell me about love," she said. She stretched her long legs out in front of her, crossing her ankles. Her cowboy boots were scuffed. "What is it like? I've forgotten." Jo's husband was a filmmaker. Kate had been the sole bridesmaid at their tiny wedding. Rob was away in Europe for five months now, shooting footage, which was why he was not here today. He made documentaries that earned critical acclaim but not much money, though he got the occasional grant. Jo mailed him poems written on the backs of postcards, and they Skyped, but the time difference and his cheap Lisbon hotel's unreliable internet made it hard.

"Not love. You mean sex," Kate said.

"Yes," Jo said. "I suppose I do."

"Now, love: love kills slowly."

"That much we know," Jo agreed.

Shortly before Valentine's Day, Jo's mother had mailed her a makeup kit in cardboard packaging with this slogan printed in eighties-style black cursive across a bright purple background. Jo tore off the slogan and deposited it in Kate's mailbox one Sunday morning, a note scrawled on the plain cardboard side: "Stopped by. You weren't here. Turn over for sound advice!"

"Can I ask you something weird? A weird favor?" Jo said, leaning forward.

"Sure."

"Look at my nose? Here?" Jo pointed to a mole.

"Okay?"

"Does it look—significant?"

Kate examined it. The mole was shaped like South America, the bottom half thinning out and hooking to the right.

"Define significant."

"Like it's changed?" Jo laughed. "Not that you've examined this particular mole on my nose before. I don't know. Stupid question. Irregular?"

"Maybe a little."

Jo sat back. "I'm turning into a hypochondriac! I'm going to go in and have it looked at, I guess."

"Does skin cancer run in your family?"

"No. We tend toward illnesses of the spleen. Hypomania, displaced rage." Jo sighed. "But my mother always said I was the boring one, that I lacked imagination. Maybe skin cancer it is for me."

Kate wrote the name of her dermatologist on a loose magazine subscription slip and, below, the number, copied from her telephone. "If you need a recommendation, I like Dr. McKiver. She's brisk and pleasant."

"Great," Jo said wryly. "Brisk and pleasant. Nonjudgmental too, I hope. If I have skin cancer of the nose, I want to use it as an excuse to get the nose job I dreamed of as a girl. I'll get a pixie cut too and come out looking like Audrey Hepburn."

"I'd miss your old nose," Kate said. Jo's nose was thin and aristocratic, sloped down and tapered like a spoon.

The nurse called Jo back for the procedure, chart in hand. Jo gave Kate a little wave. "Goodbye for now," she said, rising.

"You won't feel a thing," said Kate.

"That's what scares me," Jo replied, but with a smile, to maintain plausible deniability.

The procedure was quick. Kate read a magazine in the waiting room. Coming out of anesthesia, Jo was sweet and dopey. She held Kate's hand. She kept trying to tell a joke and forgetting the punch line. It had to do with a priest; that was as far as she could get. Her short-term memory of thirty seconds meant that twice a minute she would smile a slow, astonished smile and say with wonder to Kate, "*You're* here?"

If Jo had cancer, Kate would like to volunteer to die in her place.

• • •

On Saturday, Eli had to go out with a visiting scholar from Brazil to help him collect samples. The subject of the scholar's investigations was the death of saltwater marsh grasses in the swamplands west of New Orleans. Low-lying, uncultivated areas at the bottom of the country became pools of toxicity. The marsh grasses leached household chemicals and runoff pesticides from the groundwater. But the scholar's hypothesis about what was causing the miles of dead grasses was even more pernicious: depleted petroleum deposits and missing saline formation water, pumped out by oil companies. The land collapsed from beneath. When the marsh grasses withered, the wetlands withered. In aerial surveys the brown patches of dead grass looked like tea stains. Displaced birds flew toward the cities and nested there: the pileated woodpecker, the white ibis.

Meanwhile, red algae bloomed off the southwest Florida coast. Dead manatees were washing up on shore; they ate the algae, which poisoned them. So far, the newspaper said, the official death toll was two hundred and forty-one, and the algae was getting worse. Phosphorus from fertilizer, Eli told Kate when she read this to him over breakfast, plus higher temperatures.

Kate returned to reading the story. It was agitating her.

Eli had made blueberry pancakes with walnuts, her favorite breakfast. He put a hot stack of pancakes on a plate for her, which he set next to a jar of raspberry jam and bottle of maple syrup, then served himself.

Sitting, he drew a chair close, touched her arm. "Would you ever consider . . . ," he began.

Kate put down the paper. These were not the words she had been expecting to hear this morning, and, at the same time, they were the words she had been panicking over. She concentrated on keeping her face still and waited to see how he would complete the sentence. Marriage? Children? She felt the way she did when a student approached, about to ask yet another unanswerable question. Just down the hall, I think, she would tell him. If you don't see it, ask the administrative assistant.

He gazed at the stove, smoke from the pancakes dissipating in a blue haze, and returned his gaze to her face. "Going in on a cell phone plan with me?"

Her relief was huge. "It would depend."

"On what?"

"The carrier."

"The carrier of your choice."

He smiled, and she felt an admiration for him, followed by a pang of love. He was so practical. She was always drifting off into too theoretical realms. He rolled up his sleeves and waded into the water and collected a sample right here on earth, the place they did, after all, live.

In her relief, she relaxed, and, relaxed, she opened her mouth to tell him how she felt, this sudden adoration, but instead what came out was "I found the ring."

"You did?" he said, his voice surprised.

"It was an accident," she added quickly.

He adopted the pained squint he wore out on the bayou water when the sun hit his eyes directly.

"I was planning to ask you on my birthday."

"Your birthday?"

"What better present could there be?"

She could think of a few.

"Did you like the ring?" he asked.

She kept quiet; she had not. Or maybe she just couldn't imagine wearing an engagement ring at all.

"The ring isn't important," he continued. He was hurt, and he disliked it immensely when a plan of his failed, but he was struggling to get over it, to keep his voice light. "We can choose a new one together."

"We have to choose a cell phone carrier first."

"This isn't how I imagined this conversation going," he said. He rose, kissed her once, showily, to cheer her up, and once for real. "Let's talk about this later." She hated herself for hurting him. Why did she have to ruin things? But it had felt like a desire to be close to him, not to antagonize. Seeing her expression, he continued, "Don't worry about it. We'll figure things out." She nodded, though she wasn't sure if she should believe him.

"There are more pancakes if you want them," he said on his way out the door. "And," he added, "maybe you should stop reading about the manatees. I don't want you sitting here by yourself while I'm gone, thinking about how the world is about to end."

Later that day, she called Jo and left a message. She asked if Jo wanted to get coffee that afternoon or a drink that evening, since Eli was having dinner with the scholar, but by four p.m. she hadn't heard back. This made her impatient. She wanted to tell Jo about the ring, and to inquire about the test results. Surely by now Jo would have heard; the doctor had said he would call. Jo was private, not the type to report back, so Kate would likely have to ask. Restless, she put on rain boots and Eli's old blue sweatshirt, rolling the sleeves, and went for a walk around the lakes near campus. The sky was cloudy. At five, unable to wait any longer, she took shelter from the light drizzle, and, standing beneath the overpass, called Jo again. The pigeons huddled in the high-up nooks of the structure, immune to the hollow, thundering noise of the traffic above.

"Hello?" Jo's voice said, a little foggy—or was it the connection? The muffled whoosh of the cars overhead echoed off concrete.

"Is Apparel and Merchandising an actual major?" she asked.

Earlier that semester, she had tried to help a student majoring in this subject choose a topic for a research essay. "What are the controversies in the field?" she had asked the girl. "What current debates do you find most interesting?" The girl had looked at her in confusion before saying in a slow but friendly way, with a dose of pity, "I mean, it's just *clothes*."

"No," Jo said, firmly. "Apparel and Merchandising is not a major. Entrepreneurship is not a major. Social Drinking is not a major."

"Entrepreneurship."

"The truly dismal science."

"So when do you get the results?" Kate asked.

Jo was quiet.

"Didn't the doctor say he'd call?"

"His office called. I have to go in and talk to him. His next opening isn't for two weeks."

"He misses you!" Kate said.

"Or I have cancer."

"You don't have cancer." She tried to sound certain. "You're too young. You're too beautiful. Besides that, you're a newlywed and a poet. It would be a Lifetime movie."

A soft sigh. "Broke as a joke," Jo said. "My mother used to say that to me. Who says that? Was she trying to be some wisecracking mobster tough guy? She grew up in *Connecticut*."

"Is there anything I can do?"

"I talked to Rob. He thinks I shouldn't worry. It's probably nothing. But there was blood last night where there shouldn't be. It's alarming, you know?"

"God, Jo."

Jo paused, said, "You mentioned in your message having news?"

"Oh, yeah—it's nothing big."

"Tell me! I could use a distraction."

Kate hesitated. "I found a ring. An engagement ring."

"What?" Jo's voice was happy, excited.

"I know. But I wasn't supposed to find it, and I told Eli."

Now Jo's voice became cautious. "What exactly did you tell him?"

"Only that I found it. I'm not sure why. It was some small part of myself, a part that wanted to spoil things, I think."

"No."

"Yes."

"But he adores you, and you adore him. You two seem destined."

"Maybe I'm not ready. Maybe it's too soon."

"How many years has it been? Three?"

"A little more."

"Three years isn't nothing. Rob and I had been together eighteen months."

"So what do I do?"

"It sounds like you have two real options: marry him or break up."

Overhead traffic rumbled. A frayed rope swayed from a cement beam. It had a sinister look, and she could not imagine its original purpose. One thing she knew: not for nothing did the sunsets in Baton Rouge rival those in LA. The air was filthy, the pinks and oranges vibrant and deep, like a lily or marigold, or a chemical burn.

A ring had entered the house. It was a small bomb, a potentiality. What else entered a house? A child. A bride. A plague.

Her heart sounded in her chest, tapping out a staccato rhythm. From the Italian for *detached*, she remembered her fifth-grade piano teacher saying: each stroke separate. Like the black dot set above or below the round musical notes.

She went for a run around the lakes. It had been a long time since she'd run. High in the cypress trees, the birds creaked like leather. She breathed shallowly, through her nose: the wrong way. She listed each person with whom she had had sex, chronologically and then in descending order of age. The oldest was now forty-seven. The youngest was thirty.

Eli suggested they drive to New Orleans, see if they could find a ring she liked. They began in the less expensive antique jewelry stores on Royal Street, worked their way up to the pricier stores near Esplanade. The salespeople were attentive, eager. They offered her drinks: champagne, wine, beer, a whole array of alcoholic beverages. They praised and congratulated her, told her how happy she must be, and they turned to Eli, congratulated him on his fine choice of fiancée, as though he had ordered her from a menu. Next came a litany of questions. Question after question about what she imagined and desired in the way of a ring, a wedding, a life. Questions she had not ever considered. Questions she had considered, but had failed to resolve.

Did she want to see what this diamond looked like in natural light? Dutifully, she followed the woman to the street. It looked like . . . a diamond. Did she want, just for fun, to see a *bigger* diamond? The saleswoman emerged from the storeroom, the new stone pinched between black tweezers like a specimen. It looked like—yes—a bigger diamond! They escaped, entered another store; the questions did not stop. Did she want to put her hand on a black background, beneath this special camera, for a high-resolution picture, a picture the store would email to her? Did she want to take a brochure about the diamond-buying process? A business card, just in case? Did she want to try on an enormous ruby ring worth a half million dollars?

This last offer was made at their final stop. The rings here drew tourists.

The man slid the ring on her finger.

It was heavy. She felt like Cleopatra.

"The ruby is called 'dove's blood,'" he told her, and she thought of how the doctor had shown Jo the initial test results, a grainy black-and-white image of her organs called up on a computer monitor, to show where the blood was leaking: here, and here.

She did not want any of it.

"Thank you," she said, handing back the ring, and on the street, to Eli: "I think I hate America. I think I'm a socialist."

"You don't hate America. But you might be a socialist."

"Maybe I don't want a ring."

"Let's sleep on it," he said. "It's like cafeteria food: nothing looks appealing in such big quantities."

"That's the problem with marriage. Licenses! It's a joke. They'll give one to anybody over, what, fifteen or something, depending on the state?"

"Human rights and all that."

"Which I support. But maybe marriage should be a privilege. Or, you know, handled through a lottery system."

"That philosophy might be at cross-purposes with your new commitment to socialism," he said. "Or," he added, "on second thought, totally congruent with its more virulent forms." But he gave her hand a squeeze.

· · ·

Later that week, Kate and Jo met for coffee, an invitation extended by Jo in the form of a note left on Kate's desk. The student union, with its independent coffee stand, was undergoing renovation. They had to go to Starbucks. Kate missed the student who had staffed the coffee stand in the afternoons, a bookish girl who rang customers up with a paperback open by the register, her finger marking her place on the page. Once, Kate had asked what she was reading, and the girl flipped over the book to show the cover of *Absalom, Absalom!* In a city where Kate had asked the manager at Barnes & Noble where she might find a memoir shelved, only to watch him type "Memoir" in the title field of his computer database—no, she had explained, it was a genre, or a subgenre, not a title, at which point he directed her to the fiction section—seeing a person reading Faulkner pleased her. She had taken a modern American literature seminar her senior year at Williams. She hadn't much liked that book, but she enjoyed the kinship she felt with the girl.

Over their coffees, Kate and Jo discussed the man who evangelized outside the student union. He distributed yellow pamphlets written in the second person and illustrated with a pair of stick figures, one male and one female, likeable, everyday people who enjoyed having a good time, drinking and dancing and cavorting, but who at the end—spoiler alert!—went to hell. Hell! It seemed like an awfully steep price to pay for a daiquiri and a turn around the dance floor.

"I keep hoping it will turn out differently," Kate said.

"It won't," said Jo.

Since the call from the doctor's office, she had turned fatalistic.

"So do you want to be my bridesmaid?" Kate asked.

"Are you engaged?" Jo said, perking up.

"No, not yet."

"But you're lining up your wedding party?" Jo studied her the way she might a student with no particular aptitude or evidence of scholarly commitment who expressed an interest in graduate studies.

"Not the party," Kate said, feeling suddenly shy and confused, "just you."

"Okay," Jo said slowly, stirring her coffee. "I mean, *of course*. And that goes for whenever you get married and whomever you marry."

"I thought you liked Eli."

"I do!"

"You said you thought we were destined to be together."

"Well, yes and no."

"What do you mean, yes and no?"

"You seem to be unsure, that's all," Jo said. She rarely gave advice. Now, though, she leaned back and scrutinized Kate's face. "He's terrific, you're terrific together, but, you know. It's like that thing I had with the archeologist, the one who was such a good cook. He was great. The sex was great. He used to make these incredible chicken tagines with pink olives, and he was so sweet to me. We moved in together. Then I kissed a friend of his in our kitchen. He was outside saying goodbye to another friend, and he saw me through the window. I was a little stoned, and I used that as an excuse. It was just an excuse, though. Three months later, I knew."

"Meaning?"

"Break up with him now if you know that's what you want."

"We can't break up," Kate joked. "We just signed a lease renewal. Can you imagine the trouble?"

But when Jo spoke, she was serious. "If you don't want to marry him, it will be less trouble in the long run. You have to ask yourself: which is the better trouble to have?" Jo continued to study Kate's face, which Kate tried to make neutral, though she was worried that this was coming across as hostility to the argument, or, worse, to Jo herself. "I've been thinking about our conversation all week," Jo continued, "and I want to say this: if you want to marry him, you should."

"Okay."

"But if you don't want to marry him, admit it to yourself now. It's the only kind thing to do. Otherwise, you'll just break his heart over time, in a slow way."

"What are you trying to say?"

"People lie to themselves all the time."

"And you think I am?"

"I think that when marriage is involved, sometimes we want to live a life that is scripted by the world, not by our own desires."

"And when Rob asked you, you were totally sure."

"I was," Jo said, her voice measured but firm. "And I think that if you're honest with yourself, you'll discover that you know what you want, too.

"When I was dating Samantha"—this was Jo's ex-girlfriend, with whom she had lived in Chelsea for a few years while she was at Columbia—"I told myself we could have a future together, even though she was too much for me. Too much swagger, too much ambition. She was sexy and she was exciting and she made a ton of money, but I couldn't keep up, or I didn't want to. She wanted an apartment in the city and a house upstate, dinner parties every weekend, and I wanted a quieter life. We all lie to ourselves sometimes, especially when telling that lie might make our lives easier. Just be sure this isn't one of those times, because it's too serious."

Jo called the next afternoon, a balmy, clear-skied Friday in mid-April. Neither had to be on campus. The call was a surprise; Jo usually texted, if anything. On the phone, her voice sounded subdued. Jo asked if Kate wanted to come over and sit on the porch a bit, take advantage of the beautiful weather. Kate didn't know what to make of this; was it a casual invitation or was there something urgent on Jo's mind she didn't want to discuss on the telephone? She said yes and, though Jo's rebuke still smarted, walked the ten blocks to Jo's apartment as fast as she could. She was a little out of breath when she arrived, and she waited a minute before ringing the doorbell.

When Jo answered the door, she looked like her usual self, if a bit wan in the dim interior light. Her hair was braided and she wore yoga pants.

"Iced tea?" Jo asked. "Or I have water."

"Iced tea," Kate said.

She took the cool glass Jo offered. On the porch, they sat on the swing, pushing it lightly with the balls of their feet. The porch was painted white above gray floorboards, the ceiling done in robin's egg blue: a minor, cloudless sky. Kate tilted her head back and imagined the blue growing lighter with the sun's emergence, the sun shining down. The actual sun was sinking to the west behind their neighborhood, shadows elongated on the dry April grass.

"Do you ever wish you understood astronomy?" she asked.

"All the time," Jo said.

"All these systems behind the world, keeping order, and I hardly understand a single one of them."

"You understand a few."

"Pieces," she conceded. "Some aspects of science, literature, language—a little bit. I wish I knew a foreign language, like you. It feels like such a failing that I can only speak one."

"I am alarmed by what I don't know," Jo said. "The other day I lit a match and I thought, I don't know what fire is. What is fire?"

"A plasma. Fourth state of matter."

"I thought matter only had three states."

"In a way it's true: plasma is an ionized gas. It's actually the most common state of matter."

"And you say you don't understand anything." Jo sipped her iced tea. "I talked to the doctor."

"And?"

"He said I'm okay."

"Thank god."

"Or more or less okay."

"What does that mean?"

"It might be colitis or it might be Crohn's disease."

"But not cancer."

"Not cancer."

"And these other things are treatable?"

"Yeah. He gave me a specific diet, medication."

"This is good! Good news. Not ideal, but good."

"Good." Jo looked off in the distance. "Manageable. But it makes you think, god, this is the start: my body is going to fall apart." She paused, began again: "The dermatologist called. She didn't ask me to come in. She told me over the phone: it's malignant."

"You're kidding."

"No. I made an appointment for May 5."

"I can drive you if you need."

"That would help."

"So the dermatologist removes the mole and that's it? Or . . . what?"

"She said she doesn't think it's spread, so yeah. She removes it, and we monitor it and make sure nothing comes back and nothing new appears. Unless it's already in my lymph nodes, which is unlikely, but not impossible."

"And then?"

"Then the prognosis wouldn't be great."

Kate felt overcome. She gave Jo a hug. Jo hugged her back, stiffly, not leaning in, and Kate pulled away and patted her arm: two awkward bodies not meeting the way they should, failing to reach the fourth state of matter. "Sorry," Kate said. "Sorry, sorry."

For Eli's birthday they took a boat out on the Atchafalaya Basin through the warm, humid afternoon. He drove the motorboat. As they motored into the thicket of old-growth cypress trees, the waterway became thin. It looked like a hedge maze. Overhead, tree cover made a cathedral. Birds flew up across the path. Cypress trees had been heavily logged, first by French and Spanish and Acadian settlers for lumber and later for mulch by WalMart and Home Depot. Such logging had long been illegal, but the state agency responsible for enforcement had limited resources, including, until recently, not a single helicopter, which was the only way one could see into the swamps. The surviving trees were moss-covered beauties, hoary and skeletal and monolithic.

"I've been thinking," he said, "you've been tense about this engagement business. If it isn't fun, we're doing it wrong."

She felt her eyes tear up.

"I cannot believe," she said, "that I can't even do this right."

"Come here," he said. She climbed across the seat and sat on his lap, put her head on his chest. Their skin was sticky. His armpits smelled like deodorant and the clean, sweet tang of new sweat, and she inhaled and inhaled. "That's it," he said. He rubbed small circles on her back, below the small, sharp bone of her shoulder. He pushed on it with his thumb, finding the hardness.

"Happy birthday," she said. "I love you."

"I know," he said.

"I'm scared, I guess. Is that a totally shitty thing to hear?"

"I'm not going to lie: it's not ideal," he said. "But it is pretty normal. I mean, this is one of the biggest decisions we'll make in our lives. When you think about it, it's not rational *not* to be scared. Which makes you the more rational one."

"Besides," he continued, "it's no surprise: you question everything. Nothing's easy for you, because nothing's a given. It's kind of a pain in the ass sometimes, but that's okay. I've learned to live with it. In fact, it's part of why I love you."

"You're crazy. It's a character flaw, not a reason to love me."

"And yet," he said, "I do."

The next day, Kate and Eli went to Forever 21. Getting a fake ring was her idea: this way, she could try it out, see how she felt. They bought a yellow gold ring with a small diamond, made of plastic, and a ring shaped like a wolf's head. In the mall's florescent light, drinking milkshakes from the food court, she felt a small surge of hope. "Are you really sure you want to marry me?" she asked. "Yes," Eli said. "Most things are, at best, theories. But not this. This is true."

The night before Jo's surgery, Kate and Eli were reading in bed. They each examined their media of choice: for her, a creased copy of the *New York Times Magazine* left over from the weekend; for him, his iPad. He enlarged an image, tapped the screen, paused an ad as the horns of the jingle began to play. She glanced over. The screen cast light across the bedspread and glazed his cheekbones white. His absorption was total. She may as well be looking at the moon.

A text broke his reverie. With a sigh, he set the screen aside and took up a report he had to read for work.

"How's the coast?" she asked him.

"The coast," he said, "is fucked." He highlighted a sentence in the report. The highlighter squeaked on the paper, a deep yellow pool forming where the tip caught.

"Still?"

"Still."

His hand lay on the blanket. She took it and held it.

"Is everything fucked?"

"No," he said. "Everything is not fucked."

She admired his confidence. She liked to watch him in these moments to see how it was achieved, the way one might watch those orange Japanese beetles fly in a stuttering way on their improbable wings.

"How do you know?"

"I just do."

She felt relief. She had it on good authority that despite all appearances to the contrary, the world was not done in. A scientist had told her so.

Before the surgery, Kate gave Jo her fake engagement ring. "For good luck," she said.

"They said to remove all jewelry before going in, I think," Jo said.

"Keep it in your pocket."

"I'm pretty sure I have to change into a robe," said Jo, but she slipped the ring into the pocket of her jeans.

In *Absalom, Absalom!* one character's gravestone had been replaced with a new one because he'd done an awful thing. Only his name and birth and death date remained. No beloved. No husband, no father. No cherished.

The image had struck Kate as tragic both because it embodied an inadequate attempt to right a terrible wrong and because it pointed to a person's ultimate powerlessness in the face of death.

Write what you might in stone, it didn't matter. Once you died, you had no say. Another good reason not to do it.

After the surgery Jo did in fact look like she'd had a nose job: her nose was wrapped in a cocoon of white gauze and taped across the bridge. Bruising had begun around her right cheekbone. The miracles of local anesthetics meant Jo was lucid this time and not so easily astonished.

"Brisk and pleasant and took half my nose," Jo said, when the nurse wheeled her out.

"What happened?"

"The edge was irregular. She had to go deeper than she'd thought."

"So the ring wasn't good luck."

"I didn't die."

"You didn't die."

"But I am disfigured. She said we'd talk about scheduling reconstructive surgery once the bandages come off."

"Not half your nose."

"No. I'm exaggerating to cheer myself up."

Kate accelerated through a yellow light, glancing at Jo, who had tilted her seat back and reclined, staring up at the unlit dome with sunglasses on, like a film star. "This will give your nose character."

"You sound like my mother."

"Broke as a joke."

"Love kills slowly," said Jo, and closed her eyes.

At Jo's door, Kate asked if Jo wanted her to come in. "Tell me what I can get you. A movie to watch, a magazine, trashy French onion dip?"

"Not a thing," Jo said. "I don't need a thing. I think I want to sleep."

Kate turned to go. "Here," Jo said, handing her back the ring. "I'm sorry for what I said before. You should marry him. I don't know why I was being so cynical. Whenever he unearths the new ring and asks you, you should say yes."

"Love kills slowly," Kate said.

"Always," Jo said. "Always."

Desert Light

THE WEDDING IS tomorrow, if we don't call it off. Our families are flying into Albuquerque, and if we do decide to call it off, we'll all be stuck in the New Mexican desert on a plot of land without electricity, already not ideal and less so if plans change and the reason they have come all this way evaporates. But I don't think we will, though last night, overcome with doubt, I threatened to do exactly that, and Eli had to talk to me for a long time to convince me otherwise, pointing out that we are doing this for ourselves, and whoever wants to be there can come, and the rest of them will at least know they had the chance, and we can't do it wrong, there is no such thing. I cried for a little while into his shirt, snot running down my face, and asked if he still wanted to marry me, and he said yes, the answer was always going to be yes.

"What if we get divorced," I say now.

"We won't."

"But if we do, would you still love me? Or would you be angry with me, hate me, feel some need to punish me?"

"I wouldn't do that."

"Are you sure?"

"Why are we talking about this?" he says, and I tell him what my friend Sylvie has said, that you should only marry a person you could live with being divorced from, if it came to that.

"I have an idea," he says, "let's stop imagining our postdivorce life today, the day before our wedding."

"But I can't," I say, and he sighs and says, "Let's go get ice cream before everyone gets here. Maybe it will help distract you."

And though it is only 10 a.m., we drive into Santa Fe and get ice cream cones and eat them, dripping down our wrists, in the sun.

What no one knows except Eli is that our wedding has been planned so hastily, invitations sent to the fifteen people we've invited less than a month beforehand, because I am pregnant, and I'd thought I didn't need to be married to Eli to have a baby with him, but it turns out that I really, really do. And Eli, the good thing about Eli, the truly indispensable thing, is that when I need something, I tell him, and he listens and says, "If it's what you need, we'll figure it out," and then he begins making plans.

Yesterday afternoon, we flew into Santa Fe, though the airport is small, and rented a car. Driving in, we realized how remote it is, and our cell phones stopped getting service as we wound along the high, narrow mountain roads with spectacular drops, the canyons rust-colored, striated like shells, cliffs plunging down at dizzyingly steep angles, the landscape a little like Tucson but with the drama turned way up. Sylvie had offered to pick us up, but the thought of being stranded there on her family's land, dependent on everyone else in our lives to make things work, was too much for me, so we got a little white Toyota hybrid that keeps scaring me by ceasing to make noise, my stomach dropping at the thought the car has suddenly lost power while we are navigating these twisty roads. Sylvie met us at the house, grilled us whitefish for dinner, and we stayed up late talking to her around a bonfire outside, the wood snapping and popping, my long hair, grown out since I left Tucson, holding and radiating the earthy, pungent smell of smoke, so that when we went to bed, I had to wind it into a knot, away from my face.

"What's that *smell*," Eli said, climbing under the covers, and I said, "Me, unfortunately." After a minute in the dark, he said, "I kind of like it." "I could take a shower now," I said, and though he said it didn't bother him, to stay in bed, I got up and rinsed off in the little outdoor shower stall so I wouldn't disturb Sylvie, who slept by the indoor bathroom, my clean hair dripping on the pillow beside Eli, totally knocked out from the drive when I got back. But then I woke him, reached for him under the covers, and he mumbled a little incoherently, and we had sex, quietly, no birth control needed, which felt wrong to me, dangerous and irresponsible and therefore hot, even though I was already pregnant.

"Let's do it again," I murmured when we were done, and he said, "Sure," still half-asleep, and pulled me to him and shut his eyes and was gone, too tired to respond or having heard me wrong, but when I woke in the middle of the night, he was holding my hand.

The ceremony will take place on Sylvie's parents' land, where they've built a simple house and a few cabins, all of which run on solar power. They're surgeons who live in San Francisco, and this is their escape, where they come when they have time off and can't take the city anymore.

We spend the rest of the morning looking around for a suitable spot, and we find one, a little clearing by a knotty pinyon tree. Our families arrive midafternoon, his around 3 p.m., having flown in from Los Angeles, and mine an hour later, my mother and sister and my niece, Lola, who is seven and a total force of nature, who this year starred in the school play even though the role was originally for a boy—the play was an adaption of *James and the Giant Peach*—and who told me the last time we Skyped that she wanted to have a call-in radio show called *All Ears* so she could answer the telephone by saying, "Hello, this is *All Ears*, and I'm *all ears*." When they arrive, my mother and sister look exhausted, but Lola is excited and carrying a small canvas tote bag that moves, and her first words to me are, "Aunt Kate, I got a puppy!"

"A puppy?" I say stupidly, and Agnes, as she is hugging me, says, "We got this puppy from a guy at the airport who was giving them away . . . I hope that's okay, she just loved it so much, I couldn't say no," and all I can do is hope that Sylvie won't mind a puppy wandering around her parents' place, which is rustic but exactingly decorated.

"Don't you love him?" Lola asks, holding up the squirming puppy, and he is cute, all white with black markings on his face and a black spot on his right haunch and dark, inquisitive eyes.

"It was that or a baby goat," my mother says. "She's wanted a goat for months."

"I still want a goat," Lola clarifies. "I'm going to name him Charles."

"Maybe Charles could be the puppy's name," Eli says kindly, sensing that no one in my family is going to break the news to Lola that she is not getting a baby goat, and she says, "No, the puppy's name is Rutabaga." "We're going to change it," my sister mouths, but the puppy already seems to respond, ears rising at his new name. "Might be too late for that," my mother says, loud enough to alert Lola, and she looks over at us. I shrug and smile, and she smiles back, briefly, eyes flickering over us, trying to puzzle out what the adults have decided she is not yet allowed to know.

I help Agnes unpack, and she hangs up the dress she is going to wear tomorrow, a peach silk dress. "I like this," I say to Agnes.

"Oh, I borrowed it," she says, and I think about how it feels like my whole life is borrowed, like there is nothing to tether me to the earth, and then I feel a wave of nausea, and I think, Well, now there is.

"What friends of yours are coming?" she asks, and I tell her that Jo, whom she hasn't met, is traveling in Croatia with her husband and couldn't come, though she sent me a poem she'd written for the occasion to be read aloud at the ceremony, but that Esme is flying in that evening, an unexpected bit of kindness that surprised me more than anything else about this wedding, except maybe my own nerves.

"How does Lola like her dress?" I ask. She is our flower girl, and we sent her a white dress to wear.

"She's . . . modified it," my sister says.

"Modified?"

My sister produces the dress from her suitcase. It looks normal, and then she turns it around, and there, pinned to it, is a little cloth tail. "It's a goat tail," my sister says, watching my face for signs of displeasure. "Mom helped her make it." Agnes and Lola live with my mother now, since Agnes and Tully have split up and Agnes's office job, though stable, doesn't pay enough, and my mother likes having the company. "I hope she brought horns," I say, and my sister says, relieved, "Actually, she did."

So far, a few things are settled: we have the wedding rings and Eli's suit, and we are going to have a Quaker-style ceremony, because we went to a friend's on the Cape and liked how laid-back it was, how much less it felt like some big performance. What I don't yet have in my possession is the dress I am going to wear. If my mother's wedding dress were an option, I might have worn it, but she'd worn a dress she'd borrowed from a neighbor, and who knew where that dress was now, or that neighbor, for that matter, so, after looking around for something I didn't hate and failing to find it, I've taken Esme up on her offer to bring a dress I can borrow from her. My mother borrowed her dress, I'll borrow mine: it's a nice symmetry, but now that I'm thinking it all through, it's also beginning to seem like a terrible idea.

When Esme arrives, she seems pleased by the setup. "It's so rustic, I love it," she says, and then, walking by the outdoor shower, "That's not the only shower, right?" "No, there's a real bathroom," I tell her, and she is visibly relieved.

Esme will be staying in the nicest of the cabins, with my family staying in the house itself. Sylvie comes in to show her around, dressed in wide-legged linen pants and Birkenstocks, her hair up in a scarf, and I can see Esme assessing her, thinking that she's a little too bohemian, a little too crunchy, but she is polite and thanks Sylvie for hosting her, says nothing about the lack of an electrical outlet in the cabin, lit with a camping lantern. She does, however, ask if there is a nearby place to get an espresso, and Sylvie tells her that she'd have to drive into Santa Fe, which isn't exactly near. Esme nods sanguinely and takes out her phone, which of course doesn't get reception.

"I'll give you a map," Sylvie says.

"I can just drink regular coffee," Esme says, a bit grandly, but Sylvie is unfazed.

"Will your mom and sister want to be here for the unveiling of the dress?" Esme asks, and I say, "Oh, I doubt they'll care," so, with me and Sylvie standing around, she unzips the garment bag she has carried from Connecticut on the plane, and there it is, a long white cotton dress she insisted was too casual, which I am relieved to see has been transported safely and looks like it did when she held it up on Skype, and, behind it, her own wedding dress. "I brought mine as a surprise!" she says. "In case you wanted to wear something nicer." It is beautiful, if a chrysanthemum is your idea of beauty, a ton of tulle, totally inappropriate for the setting, which does not call for a ball gown that floats despite weighing a good ten pounds. It is a dumbbell in fabric form. I try them both on, and, seeing me in her own dress, Esme says, "Oh, you *have* to wear that one," but I can't breathe in it, and, although she is disappointed and insists I should think about it overnight, I tell her that I'll wear the other one, like we'd agreed.

"You don't want to do something you'd regret," she says threateningly, and I understand, briefly, what it is for other people to have mothers.

"I don't think I'll regret it," I say, but gently, and maybe because it is the day before my wedding day or maybe because she knows when to give up on me, Esme leaves it at that.

• • •

We've decided to announce our pregnancy at dinner. I am scared that Eli's family will be upset because they are more traditional, but they are the first to rise, smiling, and to congratulate us, his mother kissing me and whispering, "I'd hoped so," his father, a scientist too, hugging Eli in an intense way that scares me a little because Eli has hurt his back recently, and I don't want him to do anything to it before the wedding. Sylvie says "Congratulations!" and Esme says "Amazing news!" though she sounds a little shocked, and I think it's because we aren't married. But then she asks how far along I am, and I understand that the shock has to do with fear I'm sharing the news too early, which I maybe am. "Three months tomorrow," I tell her, and she asks whether we were trying very long, and I say no, and my mother, who has been very quiet, says, "I didn't know you were trying."

She hugs me, and she asks if I'm having weird food cravings, like she did, and when I say no, she tells me there's still time for them to develop. We're so similar, she says; I can pretty much bank on this happening. "I got pregnant with you without even trying," she says, "and the first trimester was easy, and then I started wanting to eat raw hamburger meat."

"That's disgusting," I say.

"My body needed iron."

"You didn't do it."

"No. Well, I had steak tartare once."

"Can't that give you toxoplasmosis?"

"It was our anniversary."

"So you risked my life."

"You turned out fine," she says. "Those were such happy days, me and your dad living in the woods together in our little house. I'd bake bread—we had that old wood stove. You never went near it once I told you it was hot. Not like your sister, who was toddling toward it with a log in her arms as soon as she could walk."

She tells me that when my sister and I were small, her life was everything she had imagined it would be. Any story can be happy or sad, I think, depending on where you begin it and where it ends, and Mary Ruefle's lines come to mind: "Some say the best thing you can do / is carry a pair of little scissors, / snip small pieces of the world / and take them home with you." Whatever has transpired between then and now, my mother is smiling, beginning to tell me a story about when I was a baby, and I'm glad she's happy.

I look around for Agnes, and Lola is sitting alone, looking excited. "You'll have a cousin," I tell her, and she says her cousin can get a dog, too, and name it Mynameis, and then we would have dogs named Mynameis Rutabaga. "What if Rutabaga comes first, though?" I ask. "Rutabaga Mynameis doesn't make sense."

"Sounds Greek," Eli says.

"What's Greek?"

"From Greece." He holds out his hand, trying to demonstrate where Greece would be if his palm were Western Europe, but she is already losing interest, asking Sylvie when we're going to eat dessert, and he switches to doing funny voices for her, which makes her giggle. Agnes is nowhere in sight, and I get up to look for her, but Eli's mother is asking me a question, and Sylvie is putting down cups for coffee, made in a French press, and Esme is giving me advice about baby names, and it's not until dinner is over that I can go look for her.

When I finally find Agnes, sitting in her cabin, she is stroking the horns Lola has brought to wear tomorrow, a nubby white fabric headband with iridescent protrusions and floppy white, pink-felt-lined ears too, I see.

"We saved you some dessert," I say. "I'm not hungry," she says. She flicks one of the ears with her index finger. "It was mint chocolate chip ice cream. When have you ever failed to be hungry for ice cream?" I sit down on the bed. "Also," I say, "I believe some congratulations are in order. Given that it's your turn to be an aunt."

"Is this about me?" she asks.

"What?" I say. "No, why would it be?"

"Because I had Lola without being married, and now you're showing me how it's done."

"That never crossed my mind."

"Why don't *you* get an abortion," she says, and when I stare at her, stunned, she stares back at me, defiantly, and starts to cry.

"That wasn't what I meant at all," I say. Because she'd been nineteen, I'd offered, if she changed her mind, to pay for an abortion or to help her find an adoption agency if that was what she wanted. I'd been worried she was being pushed into it by people who would not pay the cost of that choice themselves. "I just didn't want you to think that you had to go through with it."

She won't look at me. Finally, she says, "I'm working so hard. Nothing I do is easy now, nothing."

"I know," I say.

"I'm not sorry I had her," she says, and I say, "Of course not."

She stops crying, wipes her wet face with her hand.

"You're such a good mother," I say, and it's true.

To cheer her up, I tell her that I am a little sad to be getting married, because when I read obituaries and it is said of a woman, "She never married," I always think she must have led an interesting life, and I admire the fact that she made her way through the world on her own, even if the world doesn't make that easy, and I read about the things she'd done and think about the independence it must have taken to achieve them. That's nice, Agnes says, but she'd trade it for a break. Maybe you'll meet someone here, I say, and you can move to a ranch in New Mexico and take up rodeo riding. "More like aura reading," she says, but she smiles.

I wasn't planning to throw my bouquet tomorrow, because it always seemed like a cheesy thing to do, but now I decide that I will throw it to Agnes, toss her a little good luck in love, though luck has never been something I much trusted, and a part of me wonders whether Agnes wouldn't look good luck in the face and walk away from it, since that seems to be what she and I have both been taught to do.

Outside, the younger people sit around a chiminea, talking, as a little fire flickers, sky turning a wild, painted orange. Dusk settles around us, making the wilderness a soft blue that rustles and murmurs in the summer wind. The high desert air, full of movement, is warm and fragrant. Eli's arm is around me, his sweatshirt, which he wore to last night's bonfire, smelling like my hair did before I washed it, and he says that my mother has gone to bed, but she said to tell me good night.

Soon my sister comes out too, and Sylvie rises to find a chair for her and says something about her name being appropriate, since Agnes Martin lived in New Mexico, and my sister says, "Who?" and Sylvie goes inside and brings out a book, Agnes scowling on the cover, as if she knows we are talking about her and wants her privacy. "She came out here from New York in the sixties," Sylvie says, explaining that she was a sort of mystical weirdo who devoted herself totally to art, like a Buddhist monk, maybe in part because she was gay and in part because she was schizophrenic, who knows, but she burned all the art she made until she was forty and lived alone, happily, it seemed, outside Taos and never married, and now a gallery was named after her and her paintings were in all the major museums. Agnes and I page through the book together, minimalist abstract canvases like the land, sandy oranges and apricots, pale yellows, striations and dreamy lines.

"How did you get your name?" Sylvie asks her.

"Kate named me," Agnes says.

"Really? That's crazy."

"I was born at home, and it all happened kind of fast."

"Welcome to our childhood," I say.

"I thought New York was where a painter would want to live," Agnes says, "if they could afford it. It's interesting that she'd come here."

"Desert light," Sylvie says, and I think of our father, the postcards he sent me from the Southwest before he died, which I've never shown anyone. I decide that I will show them to my sister, after the baby is born. It would be nice to share them with someone, to tell someone, and she is the one person who might understand.

· · ·

It grows dark, and Agnes and Esme turn in, and then Sylvie says goodnight. Above, the stars are so bright it is like you'd never seen stars before. Eli shows me how to locate Pleiades and Cancer, the crab's legs, taking my face in his hands and tilting it until I see what he wants to show me. The fire burns out, and we sit quietly, listening to the darkness around us, and then a meteor shower streaks across the sky, a sparkle and dazzle, an absence.

Later, as we are falling asleep, I say, "I had no idea you knew so much about constellations."

"I'm glad you were impressed."

"Where did you learn it?"

"An app," he says sheepishly. "I wanted to impress you."

"I am impressed," I say, which is true, not because of his knowledge, but because of his honesty, his kindness. Suddenly, I feel happy, happier than I have been in so long, and I don't know where this feeling arrives from, but I am not going to turn it away. I think about Agnes Martin, alone and happy, and my sister, alone and wanting someone to share her life with, and about how, after tomorrow, I will have a new family, and I imagine what I will tell my own daughter when she arrives, just born and unknowing. I will tell her that I don't understand the world, that I have spent my whole life examining it and come to no conclusions, that the one thing I know is that I want to keep looking as long as I can.

ACKNOWLEDGMENTS

THANK YOU TO Brandon Taylor, who chose my work, and Claudia Ballard, one of this book's first and most steadfast champions, and to the staff of the University of Iowa Press. I am also grateful to my cover designer, Nicole Caputo, and to my copyeditor, Carolyn Brown.

My gratitude to the magazines and editors who first published these stories, sometimes in slightly different forms. Those stories appeared as follows: "I Met Loss the Other Day" in *Kenyon Review* and anthologized in *Readings for Writers* and *The Kenyon Review Short Fiction Chapbook*; "You Never Get It Back" in *Alaska Quarterly Review*; "Charity" in *Blue Mesa Review* and anthologized in *2018 Center for Fiction Emerging Writer Fellows: An Anthology*; "The Foothills of Tucson" in *American Short Fiction*; "Never Gotten, Never Had" in *Epoch*; "The Sea Latch" in *Missouri Review*; "At the Wrong Time, to the Wrong People" in *Narrative*; "Seeing Clear" in *Mississippi Review*; "The Most Common State of Matter" in *Granta*; and "Desert Light" in *Literary Matters*. Special thanks to Luke Neima, David Lynn, Adeena Reitberger, Rebecca Markovits, Nate Brown, Michael Koch, Ronald Spatz, Tom Jenks, Michael Croley, Andrew Malan Milward, Speer Morgan, Evelyn Somers, Melanie Unruh, Ernest Suarez, and Ryan Wilson.

Thank you to Alice Hoffman and Jessica Francis Kane for selecting stories for distinction. Thank you to the institutions that provided support of many sorts, including the Bread Loaf Writers' Conference, the Sewanee Writers' Conference, the Tin House Summer Workshop, the Virginia Center for the Creative Arts, the Kimmel Harding Nelson Center for the Arts, the Lighthouse Works, the Cuttyhunk Island Writers' Residency, Disquiet International Literary Program, Coastal Carolina University, Seton Hall University, the Centre for Interdisciplinary Studies of Society and Culture at Concordia University, and the New York State Council on the Arts.

Thank you to the Center for Fiction and my cofellows there, and to the many extraordinary writers and friends who read these stories along the way and whose own work taught me, too, including Amy Hempel, Paul Harding, Anthony Doerr, Margot Livesey, Alice McDermott, Donald Antrim, Peter Ho Davies, Christopher Tilghman, Alexi Zentner, Molly Antopol, Claire Vaye Watkins, Teddy Wayne, Caoilinn Hughes, David James Poissant, Aurelie Sheehan, Jason Brown, and Elizabeth Evans. Especially central to this collection were R. O. Kwon, Mika Taylor, Mark Polanzak, Elliott Holt, and Joseph Lee. For their friendship, support, and advice, thank you to Rajesh Parameswaran, Patricia Park, Mike Scalise, Kaitlyn Greenidge, Nathan Oates, Amy Wilkinson, Nicholas Boggs, Cutter Wood, Erin Shaw, Megan Fernandes, Joshua Neves, Paul Behrens, Jackie Gilbert, and Courtney Zoffness. Thank you to the publishers and authors who extended permission to quote their work, including Ariel Lewiton, Hannah Dela Cruz Abrams, Mary Ruefle, and Garielle Lutz.

Thank you to my mother for many things, including the Alice Munro books. Thank you to our dog, Blaze, who encouraged me to pay attention to the world with patience and curiosity and who celebrated every happy occurrence with me. And thank you to Cam Terwilliger for his intelligence, integrity, and love.

PERMISSIONS

ix. Epigraph from *Housekeeping* by Marilynne Robinson. Copyright © 1981 by Marilynne Robinson. Reprinted by permission of Farrar, Straus and Giroux. All rights reserved.

11. "You never get it back." From Ernest Hemingway, "Hills Like White Elephants," *Men Without Women*. Copyright © 1927 by Charles Scribner's Sons; copyright renewed 1955 by Ernest Hemingway. Reprinted with the permission of Scribner, a division of Simon & Schuster, Inc. All rights reserved.

121. "What stood out about him was that his life got put past him." From Gary Lutz, "Mine," *The Complete Gary Lutz*. Copyright © 2019 by Tyrant Books. Reprinted by permission of Tyrant Books. All rights reserved.

128. "Her English-speaking voice is misleading: hesitant and lilting with the nervous charm of someone who is new to a language." From an unpublished memoir by Hannah Dela Cruz Abrams. Courtesy of the author.

128. "It's like being in a tunnel. Finally I emerge onto the brilliance of the *quai*, beneath a roof of glass panels which seems to magnify the light." From James Salter, *A Sport and a Pastime*. Copyright © 1967; copyright renewed 1995 by James Salter. Reprinted by permission of Farrar, Straus and Giroux. All rights reserved.

129. "—the frightening gills, / fresh and crisp with blood, / that can cut so badly— / I thought of the coarse white flesh / packed in like feathers, / the big bones and the little bones." From Elizabeth Bishop, "The Fish." *Poems* by Elizabeth Bishop. Copyright © 2011 by the Alice H. Methfessel Trust. Reprinted by permission of Farrar, Straus and Giroux. All rights reserved.

129. "That April I felt so heavy and I went to the sauna to feel less heavy but it didn't work. I went because I wanted to remember that the heart was a muscle more than it was a metaphor: when it hurt the hurt was most often a metaphor, but when the hot-cold-hot of my rotation

from sauna to ice bath and back made it thump crazily against my ribs, that pounding was the muscle laboring to keep me alive." From Ariel Lewiton, "April Sauna," *PEN Poetry Series*, June 27, 2018, https://pen.org/april-sauna/. Courtesy of the author.

184. "Some say the best thing you can do / is carry a pair of little scissors, / snip small pieces of the world / and take them home with you." From Mary Ruefle, "How We Met," *Dunce*. Courtesy of the author.

THE IOWA SHORT FICTION AWARD AND THE JOHN SIMMONS SHORT FICTION AWARD WINNERS, 1970–2021

Lee Abbott
Wet Places at Noon

Cara Blue Adams
You Never Get It Back

Donald Anderson
Fire Road

Dianne Benedict
Shiny Objects

Marie-Helene Bertino
Safe as Houses

Will Boast
Power Ballads

David Borofka
Hints of His Mortality

Robert Boswell
Dancing in the Movies

Mark Brazaitis
The River of Lost Voices: Stories from Guatemala

Jack Cady
The Burning and Other Stories

Jennine Capó Crucet
How to Leave Hialeah

Pat Carr
The Women in the Mirror

Kathryn Chetkovich
Friendly Fire

Cyrus Colter
The Beach Umbrella

Marian Crotty
What Counts as Love

Jennifer S. Davis
Her Kind of Want

Janet Desaulniers
What You've Been Missing

Sharon Dilworth
The Long White

Susan M. Dodd
Old Wives' Tales

Merrill Feitell
Here Beneath Low-Flying Planes

Christian Felt
The Lightning Jar
James Fetler
Impossible Appetites
Starkey Flythe Jr.
Lent: The Slow Fast
Kathleen Founds
When Mystical Creatures Attack!
Sohrab Homi Fracis
Ticket to Minto: Stories of India and America
H. E. Francis
The Itinerary of Beggars
Abby Frucht
Fruit of the Month
Tereze Glück
May You Live in Interesting Times
Ivy Goodman
Heart Failure
Barbara Hamby
Lester Higata's 20th Century
Edward Hamlin
Night in Erg Chebbi and Other Stories
Ann Harleman
Happiness
Elizabeth Harris
The Ant Generator
Ryan Harty
Bring Me Your Saddest Arizona
Charles Haverty
Excommunicados
Mary Hedin
Fly Away Home
Beth Helms
American Wives
Jim Henry
Thank You for Being Concerned and Sensitive
Allegra Hyde
Of This New World
Matthew Lansburgh
Outside Is the Ocean
Lisa Lenzo
Within the Lighted City
Kathryn Ma
All That Work and Still No Boys
Renée Manfredi
Where Love Leaves Us
Susan Onthank Mates
The Good Doctor
John McNally
Troublemakers
Molly McNett
One Dog Happy
Tessa Mellas
Lungs Full of Noise
Kate Milliken
If I'd Known You Were Coming
Kevin Moffett
Permanent Visitors

Lee B. Montgomery
Whose World Is This?
Rod Val Moore
Igloo among Palms
Lucia Nevai
Star Game
Thisbe Nissen
Out of the Girls' Room and into the Night
Dan O'Brien
Eminent Domain
Philip F. O'Connor
Old Morals, Small Continents, Darker Times
Robert Oldshue
November Storm
Eileen O'Leary
Ancestry
Sondra Spatt Olsen
Traps
Elizabeth Oness
Articles of Faith
Lon Otto
A Nest of Hooks
Natalie L. M. Petesch
After the First Death There Is No Other
Marilène Phipps-Kettlewell
The Company of Heaven: Stories from Haiti
Glen Pourciau
Invite
C. E. Poverman
The Black Velvet Girl
Michael Pritchett
The Venus Tree
Nancy Reisman
House Fires
Josh Rolnick
Pulp and Paper
Sari Rosenblatt
Father Guards the Sheep
Blake Sanz
The Boundaries of Their Dwelling
Elizabeth Searle
My Body to You
Enid Shomer
Imaginary Men
Chad Simpson
Tell Everyone I Said Hi
Heather A. Slomski
The Lovers Set Down Their Spoons
Marly Swick
A Hole in the Language
Barry Targan
Harry Belten and the Mendelssohn Violin Concerto
Annabel Thomas
The Phototropic Woman
Jim Tomlinson
Things Kept, Things Left Behind

Douglas Trevor
The Thin Tear in the Fabric of Space
Laura Valeri
The Kind of Things Saints Do
Anthony Varallo
This Day in History
Ruvanee Pietersz Vilhauer
The Water Diviner and Other Stories
Don Waters
Desert Gothic
Lex Williford
Macauley's Thumb
Miles Wilson
Line of Fall
Russell Working
Resurrectionists
Emily Wortman-Wunder
Not a Thing to Comfort You
Ashley Wurzbacher
Happy Like This
Charles Wyatt
Listening to Mozart
Don Zancanella
Western Electric